By Secret Railway

By Enid LaMonte Meadowcroft

Illustrations by Dom Lupo

SCHOLASTIC BOOK SERVICES

Published by Scholastic Book Services, a division
of Scholastic Magazines, Inc., New York, N.Y.

With love to

DILLA MACBEAN

whose enthusiasm for Chicago inspired
me during the writing of this book

Copyright 1948 by Enid LaMonte Meadowcroft. This edition is
published by Scholastic Book Services, a division of Scholastic
Magazines, Inc., by arrangement with Thomas Y. Crowell
Company.

2nd printing...................................February 1967

Printed in the U.S.A.

CONTENTS

chapter 1

An Important Decision

D AVID MORGAN let the kitchen door slam behind
him and dropped an armful of wood to the floor
with a clatter.

"There you are, Nancy," he said to his twin sister,
who stood at the stove stirring a large pot of bubbling
oatmeal for breakfast. "There's enough wood to last
for a week of Sundays."

Then he lowered his voice. "You didn't tell anyone
about what happened to me in school yesterday, did
you?" he asked.

"Of course not!" Nancy exclaimed indignantly,
pushing a lock of brown hair back from her forehead.
"I promised you I wouldn't."

David squatted down and began to stack the wood

1

in the box beside the stove. After a minute he chuckled and sat back on his heels.

"You know, Nance, old lady Collins does look funny, standing up there in front of the class blinking at us through her spectacles like a big fat owl. That picture I drew looked just like her, so I can't say it didn't, can I? And she won't let me come back to school until I do say so, and tell her I'm sorry I drew it."

Nancy's blue eyes were troubled. "You should have been doing your lessons, instead of wasting your time drawing," she said, trying to sound disapproving.

David grinned rather sheepishly. "There was plenty of time to do them later," he protested. "I'm pretty fast at my lessons, Nance. It doesn't take me nearly as long to do them as it does most of the class."

"There you go again, crowing like a rooster!" Nancy exclaimed, waving an oatmealy spoon at her brother. "To hear you talk, sometimes a body'd think you figured you were the fastest boy in all Chicago. Maybe if you weren't quite so fast, Davy, your marks would be better and Mother wouldn't worry about you so much. What are you going to say to Miss Collins when you go back this morning?"

"Nothing," David replied airily. Then, growing suddenly more serious, he stood up and faced his sister.

"I'm not going back to that old school any more," he said decidedly. "I can read and write and spell, and I know all the arithmetic I need to know. It's just a waste of time to sit in that poky, dark old place over a lot of books, and I'm not going to do it another day."

"Davy!" Nancy exclaimed, staring at her brother as though he had taken leave of his senses. "If you don't go to school, what on earth are you going to do?"

"Get a job on the Water Street wharves, the way Bill Daley did last fall," David replied, feeling quite grown up and important. "Or I'll work on one of the lake steamers, maybe, or — "

"But Bill Daley is fourteen," Nancy interrupted, "and you're only twelve. Mother will never let you go to work on the wharves, or on a ship either. And Grandpa will be mad enough to eat nails if you skip school even for a day."

"Grandpa won't need to know it yet, and neither will Ma, unless you tell 'em," David said. "By the time they find it out I'll have a job and be jingling money in my pockets.

"Glory, Nance! Then they'll both be glad. I know they will. I heard Ma telling Grandpa just yesterday that Robbie needs new boots, and Peter's outgrowing his winter coat, and she didn't know how she was going to pay the man who fixed the chimney, and — "

He broke off abruptly at the sound of feet running down the hall stairs.

"Promise you won't tell anyone yet?" he whispered urgently. "Promise?"

For an instant Nancy hesitated. Then she nodded her head. Hastily taking a pile of bowls from the cupboard near the stove, she began to set them out, one by one, on the table in the center of the big room which served as kitchen, dining room, and sitting room combined. Hardly had she set the first bowl down when the door leading into the hall was flung open and two small boys burst into the room.

Seven-year-old Robbie was redheaded and freckled, but Peter, who was a year younger, looked very much like Nancy and David, with dark hair and eyes the color of the sky on a sunny day.

"Ma says I can have molasses on my oatmeal this morning," Peter announced gleefully, pulling out a chair and seating himself at the table.

Nancy shook her head. "There's not a drop in the house, Petey," she told her small brother. "Mother must have forgotten that we used the last of it in the candy we made yesterday."

Peter scowled and reached for a piece of bread. But he stopped suddenly, with his hand in mid-air, when a deep voice boomed from the doorway of a little room just off the kitchen.

"Hi there, you young rapscallion, let that bread alone until your mother gets here and the blessing's been said," the voice commanded. And Grandfather Morgan limped into the room, buttoning a worn alpaca jacket under his long white beard.

Peter put the bread down quickly and Robbie spoke up.

"Ma isn't coming yet," he drawled, leaning over to stroke Inky, the large black cat, who had just stalked out from behind the stove. "She says to tell you she has an awful toothache and didn't sleep a wink last night, and will Nancy please give us our breakfast and send us off to school early, so that she can get a nap before it's time to open the shop?"

Nancy nodded, wishing as she filled each bowl with oatmeal that there were not so much work to be done at home, so that she might go off to school with her brothers. When the porridge bowls were well filled, she put a pot of tea and a pitcher of milk on the table and announced that breakfast was ready.

David tumbled the rest of the wood helter-skelter into the woodbox and brushed the chips from his dark brown pantaloons. Everyone sat down and all heads were bowed.

"Bless this food, dear Lord," Grandfather prayed in his deep voice. "Remove, we beseech Thee, the curse of slavery from our land and give us strength to meet the troubled days that lie ahead. Amen."

"Amen," echoed Peter in a shrill little voice, and reached again for the bread.

Robbie flooded his oatmeal with milk from the big yellow pitcher. Nancy poured a cupful of steaming tea for Grandfather, while David passed the doughnuts. Everyone was hungry, and for some moments the only sounds in the room were the clattering of the boys' spoons against their bowls and the crackling of the wood fire in the large iron stove.

Then a jolly little woman, who looked just like a

grown-up Nancy, came bustling into the room, tying a blue-striped apron over her long full skirt as she crossed to the table and sat down.

"My toothache is almost gone," she announced cheerfully, "and I just couldn't stay in bed even for a catnap when I thought of Nancy with all the dishes to wash and the cookies to make and the shop to sweep out. So here I am."

David smiled uneasily at her. "I'll sweep out the shop for you, Ma, before I leave," he said, swallowing his last bite of porridge. Delighted to have an excuse to get out of the room, he jumped up, grabbed a broom from the corner near the wooden sink, and stepped into the hall, closing the door behind him.

Grandfather Morgan looked after him in surprise.

"Is the lad sick?" he asked with a twinkle in his eyes. "He remembered to fill the woodbox, his hair is combed, he's washed his face, and he's actually going to sweep out the shop without being asked to do so at least a dozen times."

Robbie giggled, and Mrs. Morgan smiled. "David's just growing up," she said, pouring herself a cup of tea.

Grandfather nodded. "That's right!" he exclaimed. "Well, I have great hopes for him now that we have a free high school here in Chicago."

Swinging around in his chair, the old gentleman spoke to Nancy, who stood at the stove, filling Robbie's bowl again with oatmeal.

"How is the lad getting on these days with his lessons, Nance?" he asked. "I've been too busy working on my book to question him, but he tells you everything. Has he been in any more trouble in school lately?"

"Well," Nancy began slowly, feeling rather guilty, and hardly knowing how to answer because of her promise to David. "I think he — "

A cry from Peter cut her short.

"My milk!" the small boy wailed, jumping up from the table to escape the flood of milk which streamed from his overturned mug. "It upset all by itself, and it's even dripping into my boots."

Nancy breathed a sigh of relief. Never before had an accident been so welcome. Snatching a dish towel, she began to mop up the puddle of milk which was spreading out over the red-checked tablecloth. Mrs. Morgan wiped off Peter's long pantaloons and high leather boots, and by the time the child was seated at the table again, Grandfather's question had been forgotten.

Meanwhile David had begun to sweep out the little store where his mother, with Nancy's help, sold cookies, cakes, bread, and candy.

Although the shop occupied the entire front of the house, it was not a large room. David could well remember the time, before his father died, when it had been the family sitting room, with a Franklin stove set in the corner between two windows and a shiny horsehair sofa against one wall. The stove was still there. But the sofa was gone. So were the four straight-backed chairs, the big rocker, the red-flowered carpet, the marble-topped table, and the oil paintings of Great-grandfather and Great-grandmother Morgan.

Now there was a wooden counter halfway down the room and a glass-covered case, filled with small trays of molasses taffy, peppermint drops, blocks of maple sugar, and licorice sticks. There were some empty trays, too, which later in the day would hold raisin cakes, current buns, gingerbread squares, and cookies of vari-ous flavors and sizes. On the shelves behind the coun-ter stood several tall glass jars, filled with lemon drops, lime drops, cinnamon balls, brown horehound, and strings of shiny rock candy.

Just outside one shop window a sign reading "Mrs. Susan Morgan — Candy and Baked Goods" swung back and forth in the wind. A bell which jangled to an-nounce the coming of customers hung over the shop door. And on the wall near the door was a big calendar with "March 1860" printed boldly under a picture of three cows in a sunny meadow.

David glanced at the calendar. "Ma forgot to change it," he thought. "March was over three days ago." And reaching up, he tore off a page for the month that was past.

That done, he finished his sweeping, opened one of the windows, and dumped the dirt outside. Next he wiped the dust from the glass case with his coat sleeve and stuck a few pieces of wood into the stove, in case his mother should want a fire. Then he leaned on his broom and listened intently.

Outside, a horsecar rattled down State Street, its bell clanging. A calf, tethered in a nearby vacant lot, bellowed mournfully. Somewhere a rooster crowed. A dog began to bark. And a man called, "Whitefish for sale — nice and fresh. Whitefish for sale . . ."

Inside, David could hear Peter wailing that he couldn't find his jacket, and Robbie asking his mother for some cookies to put with his school lunch. Then, after a moment's silence, came the sounds David was hoping to hear. Peter and Robbie were calling good-by.

"Good!" thought David. "They've gone on without me. Now they can't pester me with questions because I'm not going to school with them."

After waiting long enough for the younger boys to get well on their way, he picked up his dustpan and started for the kitchen, where Nancy was washing dishes and his mother had already begun her baking. Ten minutes later, with his midday lunch stuffed into one pocket and an arithmetic book in the other, David was ready to leave.

Mrs. Morgan looked up from the batter which she was mixing in a big yellow bowl. "Be a good boy, son," she said, reaching up to straighten David's collar. "Work hard."

"I will," David promised. "Glory, Ma! I'm going to work so hard that someday I can buy you the finest

hoopskirt in all the city. And I'll get Nancy a new bonnet and Robbie some new boots and —"

Mrs. Morgan laughed. "That day is a long way off,
I think, Davy," she said. "Now hurry up, or you'll be
late to school."

It was just at that instant that David caught Nancy's
eye. His face reddened slowly. Blurting out the word
"Good-by," he turned, ran quickly down the back steps,
and started up State Street in the direction of the
school.

But when he came to the corner of Madison Street,
he did not even look to the left, where, only a block
away, children were flocking into the big wooden
school building opposite McVicker's Theater. Dodging
in and out among the men who were hurrying to work
and the women who were going to market, he kept
straight ahead. Splashing through the mud at the

crossings, ducking under the noses of two fine dray horses that were hauling a load of water casks, and nearly bumping into a blue-coated policeman who was chasing his cap down the wind-blown street, he turned at last into Water Street.

Not until he reached this busy, narrow thoroughfare, lined with stores and warehouses, crowded with market wagons, drays, and carriages, and smelling sharply of coffee, spices, fresh-cut lumber, and fish, did he slacken his pace. Then he leaned against a lamp-post, drew a deep breath, and looked around.

Behind the buildings on the opposite side of the street rose the tall masts of the brigs and schooners which filled the Chicago River just beyond. Straight ahead, moored to the wharf at the foot of State Street, the proud paddle-wheel steamer *Lady Elgin* lay waiting for the load of mail and passengers which she would carry to various ports in Wisconsin. And a great four-masted bark, loaded heavily with wheat and sailing for England by way of the Welland Canal, nosed her way down the river in the wake of a sturdy little tug.

Lake gulls wheeled high overhead, screaming shrilly as they swooped down to snatch a fish or a bit of garbage from the murky water. Tugs whistled. Stevedores, loading an east bound vessel with bundles of hides and barrels of salt pork, called back and forth to one another as they worked. Drivers joked together and shouted orders to their horses while they filled their waiting wagons with sacks of coal from Pennsylvania, iron newly arrived from Ohio, and barrels of salt from Syracuse, New York.

David watched two red-faced Irishmen unloading from their dray big bales of cotton, which had been picked and packed in the South by Negro slaves. And he grinned to see a large yellow cat leap to the top of one of those bales and settle herself for a nap in the sun.

Then, all at once, he remembered why he was standing on South Water Street early in the morning of a school day. And with that memory he felt a sinking sensation in the pit of his stomach. It was one thing, he suddenly discovered, to stand in the kitchen, talking big to Nancy about getting a job and quite another to walk up to a man in a shipping office or on the wharves and ask for work.

"But I can't stay here on this corner all day," he told himself. "First I'll try to get work over there on the wharf where the *Queen of the West* is moored." And sticking his hands in the pockets of his pantaloons, he started slowly to cross the street.

chapter 2

Things Begin to Happen

I T WAS nearly one o'clock. Most of the people of Chicago had finished their midday meals. In the Morgans' kitchen, Mrs. Morgan was cutting slabs of warm gingerbread into squares, while, in the shop, Nancy was waiting on a little boy who had come to buy a penny's worth of peppermints.

At the Dearborn School, Peter and Robbie were wondering where David was. And David himself was walking slowly down the narrow strip of sandy beach, just east of Michigan Avenue, below the railroad station.

Although a stiff wind was blowing across the lake on the other side of the breakwater beyond the railroad trestle, the sun was warm. Except for two men sauntering toward the station, the little beach seemed deserted. David sat down on an overturned rowboat near the water's edge and tugged at the packet of lunch which he had crammed into his jacket pocket. He was just as hungry as if he had been working hard all the morning. But he hadn't.

On the wharves, in a big warehouse, and in three shipping offices he had been told that no boys were needed. In Brown's sail loft, a bowlegged old sailor had growled at him that he was nothing but a little pip-squeak who ought to be in school. And the only money he had made was seven large copper pennies, which he had earned holding the skittish horse of a fashion-ably dressed young gentleman who was engaging passage for Buffalo on a big steamer. However, David wasn't discouraged.

"I'll stay around here until it's time for school to be out," he told himself. "Then I'll go home so that Ma and Grandfather won't suspect anything, and tomor-row morning I'll start looking for work again."

Laying his packet of lunch beside him on the row-boat, he opened it and looked to see what Nancy had packed for him. There were four fat ham sandwiches, an apple with a soft spot in it, two doughnuts, and three sugar cookies. David picked up the biggest sandwich, took a bite, and stared out over the water, wishing that he were far out on the lake aboard the ship which was disappearing into the distance with her sails all filled with wind.

So absorbed did he become in imagining how he

would feel on shipboard that he did not notice someone approaching him across the sand. And he jumped
as if he had been shot when a voice close to his ear
said shyly, "Hello!"

Quickly David turned around. There, not three feet
away, was a boy a year or so older than himself — a
boy with skin which was the rich brown color of fresh-
turned earth, and with black hair curled tightly under
his torn cotton cap. "Hello," the boy said again, speaking a little louder. "What's your name?"

"David Morgan," David answered in a friendly tone,
looking curiously at the other boy. "What's yours?"

"Jim Clayton," the newcomer replied hesitantly. He
studied David thoughtfully for a long moment, as
though he were trying to decide whether or not he
could trust him. Then he slowly straddled the up-
turned bow of the boat, sat down, and eyed David's
lunch longingly.

"I is powerful hungry," he announced after a minute
of embarrassed silence. "If you can spare some of that
food, I'll give you this." Pulling a small slingshot from
the pocket of his ragged brown jacket, he held it out
toward David. "It ain't much," he confessed, "but it's
all I got."

David shook his head. "Don't want it, thank you,"
he said, swallowing a mouthful of bread and ham.
"Here, help yourself." He pushed the package of lunch
toward Jim's end of the boat, wondering as he did so
who the boy was and where he had come from so suddenly.

Jim put the slingshot back into his pocket, took a sandwich, and sank his teeth into it.

"It sure is good," he declared, with his mouth full. "I ain't had nothin' to eat since yesterday, when a man on that jiggety train give me an apple."

"What train?" David asked.

"Train from some place they calls Cairo," Jim replied, licking some ham grease from his fingers and shivering as a fresh gust of wind swept over the beach. "It's on that big old river that Kentucky is the other side of."

"Kentucky?" David repeated, with a question in his voice. Then he nodded his head knowingly.

Many times he had heard or read tales of Negro slaves who had escaped from their masters in the South and had found their way to the northern states, where slavery had been abolished long ago and where slave owning was forbidden. Dimly he remembered an exciting time, several years earlier, when his father had hidden such a runaway under a rain barrel in the back yard while a man from the South, who claimed to be the slave's owner, had searched in vain for him.

David did not recall what had happened to that particular runaway. He did know, however, that many fugitives who had reached Chicago safely had fled still farther north to Canada, where their owners could never claim them. He knew also that others had decided to remain in the city among friends, even though they ran the risk of being recaptured and taken south again.

It took courage to run away from one's master. Of that David was sure, and he looked at Jim admiringly. "Running away, aren't you?" he asked.

Jim shook his head solemnly. "No, sir," he declared firmly. "I ain't a runaway. I ain't even a slave no longer. I is free. I got a paper from Master Henry right here in my pocket that says so." He patted his jacket pocket lovingly.

"There ain't no one can ever make me a slave again," he went on proudly. "My pappy done fixed that for me. He bought me from Master Henry. Paid three hundred and ten dollars for me, too."

David whistled softly. "Jingoes, that's a lot of money, Jim!" he exclaimed, thinking at the same time how strange it was that a father should have to buy his own son. "Where did your father get it?"

"Earned it, right here in the city, all by himself," Jim announced, brushing some sand from the doughnut David had handed to him. "About four years back, my pappy run off from the plantation and came here to Chicago. An' Master Henry didn't ever even try real hard to catch him. He said it just weren't worth the trouble or the money to chase after him, 'cause my pappy is a thinkin' man, and thinkin' men don't make good slaves. They starts other slaves to thinkin', and that might stir up a ruckus, Master Henry said. So he just let my pappy go."

"Where is your father now?" David asked.

Jim's forehead wrinkled into a worried frown. "I don't know," he replied slowly. "When Master Henry give me the money to ride on the train, he told me to wait in the depot here in Chicago till my pappy came for me. But I waited and I waited, and he never did come. And pretty soon two men began lookin' at me like they thought I was a runaway. I didn't want no trouble, so I sneaked off when they wasn't lookin' and came down here and crawled under that boat over there."

Jim pointed to a small boat which lay, bottom side up, a short distance away. "I reckon I fell asleep under there," he continued. "Anyway the next thing I knew it was daylight and I was near froze to death. Then I saw you sittin' here, eatin', and you looked sort of friendly like, so I crawled out and said 'hello.' "

David grinned. "I'm glad you did," he said, for there was something about the older boy that he liked very much. "What are you going to do now?" he asked, handing Jim two of the sugar cookies.

"Find my pappy, of course," Jim replied. "Master Henry said he was workin' in some place they calls Tremont House. Can you tell me where it is?"

David nodded. "It's a big hotel on Lake Street," he said. "I've been there lots of times. Here, eat this apple while we walk along, and I'll take you there."

He gave the apple to Jim and stuffed into his own pocket the napkin in which his lunch had been wrapped. Then the two boys left the beach together.

David was bursting with questions which he wanted to ask about how it felt to be a slave, and what kind of work Jim had done in Kentucky, and whether he had any brothers or sisters, and all sorts of other things. But he didn't quite know how to begin without seeming rude and inquisitive. So he said little.

As for Jim, he was so bewildered by the sights and sounds of the city, so anxious to reach his father, and so eager to see all that there was to see that he had no desire to do much talking.

Side by side, the boys walked through a little park and up Michigan Avenue, with its fine homes surrounded by trees and wide lawns. Then they turned into Lake Street, and Jim tossed his apple core into the muddy gutter and walked closer to David.

Never before had the young lad from the South seen such a busy, noisy place. Men in high silk hats and women in wide hoopskirts and bonnets were hurrying about in the brisk April wind. Gentlemen on horseback bowed to ladies in fine carriages. Omnibuses, filled with passengers, rattled over the wood-paved street.

A newsboy cried his papers. Two little bootblacks yelled names at each other as they vied for trade on opposite corners. And bystanders were shouting advice to the driver of a big westbound covered wagon, who was trying to mend a broken wheel.

But it was the buildings which made Jim's eyes widen in astonishment. "I ain't never seen such tall houses in all my born days!" he exclaimed, gazing with awe at the four- and five-story brick buildings which stood close together on either side of the street. "Looks like they might fall over right on top of us. What for do they make 'em so high?"

David chuckled. "They're not houses," he said, as he started to cross the street. "They're all stores and offices. Hey, look out there!" He grabbed Jim's arm and pulled him out of the way of an American Express wagon which was clattering by.

"Sure do have to keep your eyes wide open in this place," Jim said breathlessly, as he started to climb a flight of wooden steps. "What for do they have so many stairs, up and down, up and down, in this here walk?"

"Because the city's too low," David explained. "They're lifting it up out of the mud — filling in the streets and even hoisting up the buildings. Look, there's the Tremont House." He pointed to a big brick building on the corner. "We'll go around to the livery stable at the back," he went on. "I've got a friend there. Maybe he can tell you where to find your father." And he ducked into an alley, with Jim close at his heels.

A little old man with a face like a dried apple sat on a stool just outside the stable, polishing a saddle. He looked up when the boys drew near and grinned at David.

"Howdy, young fellow," he cried in a thin, cracked voice. "I ain't laid eyes on you in nigh onto two weeks. Where've you been?"

"Oh, just around," David answered vaguely. Then he nudged Jim. "That's my friend, Mr. Adams, Jim," he said. "Go ahead, ask him."

Jim pulled the cotton cap from his head. "Has you

seen my pappy around here?" he asked, twisting the
cap in his hands. "His name is Jim Clayton, jes' like
mine, an' he's most as tall as that door, an' he has a
kind of crookety scar on his cheek."

Mr. Adams thoughtfully rubbed the saddle with his
polishing cloth. "Yes, I've seen him," he replied slowly.
"He used to work in the kitchen here, but he don't
now."

"Where is he?" Jim asked eagerly.

Mr. Adams blinked his eyes solemnly. "Well, boy,"
he drawled, "I sure hate to tell you this, but your good
pa has gone from this old earth forever. 'Bout ten days
ago it was, he stopped a pair of horses that was running away down Dearborn Street.

"He saved the lady and the little boy who was riding
in the carriage, all right. They never got a scratch.
Funny thing, your pa didn't get a scratch either. But
he must have hurt himself real bad someway inside,
'cause that night he couldn't do his work and said he
didn't feel good. And the next morning he was dead."

"Dead," Jim repeated miserably, "but —" He could
go no further. With his sleeve he wiped away two tears
which were trickling down his cheeks. "I ain't cryin',"
he declared, swallowing hard. "My pappy once told
me men don't never cry. I is just thinkin', tryin' to figure
out what to do next."

"You'd better get yourself out of Chicago and into
Canada on the first boat you can get aboard," Mr.
Adams advised earnestly. "Why, only yesterday
there were two hard-looking strangers right here in the

hotel trying to find a slave who had run away from some place in Mississippi and —"

"Jim doesn't need to worry about those old slave catchers," David broke in. "He's not a slave. He's got his paper that says he's free."

Then, catching the other boy's arm, he added, "Come on, Jim, my grandfather will help you. So will my mother. They'll tell you what to do." And calling back a brief word of thanks to Mr. Adams, he started up the alley with Jim close behind him.

The two boys had little to say to one another as they walked to the Morgans' home. Jim, shivering in the cold wind which cut through his thin jacket and blew into his face, was thinking unhappily about his father. David was feeling sorry for Jim. At the same time he was beginning to be very much worried about what his mother and grandfather would say when they learned he had not been in school. So scarcely a word was spoken by either boy until the two reached the house.

Then David took Jim to the little shed in the back yard, which was used as a storage place for all kinds of odds and ends.

"You wait here a minute, Jim," he told him. "I have to straighten something out with my mother and grandfather before I bring you in. Sit on that bench over there. I'll be right back."

Poor Jim, who was by this time so cold and so unhappy and so bewildered that he didn't care very much what happened to him, sank down on the bench without a word.

Closing the door softly behind him, David went up the back steps, sniffing hungrily at the odor of fresh cake which greeted him as he stepped inside the kitchen. To his amazement he found the big room empty and in great disorder. Papers and books were piled high on the table. The armchair from his grandfather's room, just off the kitchen, was filled with shirts, underwear, cravats, stockings, a shawl, and various other kinds of men's clothing.

From the sounds overhead, David felt sure that furniture was being shifted about. He was just starting up the stairs to investigate when Nancy came down, her face all red from hurrying, her hair flying in all directions, and her arms laden with bedding.

"Here," she said, thrusting her burden at David. "Take these into Grandpa's room and bring up the sheets and blankets that are on his bed."

"What's going on?" David asked wonderingly, looking at his sister over the pile of blankets.

Nancy smoothed down her hair with both hands. "We have a boarder," she announced. "He just walked into the shop and asked Mother if we had a room to rent, and he's going to have Grandpa's room and eat his breakfasts with us and pay us three dollars a week."

"Whew!" David whistled. "What's his name?"

"Snively," Nancy replied, wrinkling her nose. "He looks like a frog, and I don't like him. But Mother says three dollars is three dollars, and Grandpa says he won't mind at all sleeping up in your bed for a while. You're going to sleep down here in the kitchen on a shakedown."

She gave her brother a little push. "Hurry up, Dave," she said. "Mr. Snively will be back soon with his things, and we have so much to do." And she began to gather up some of the clothing which lay on the chair.

"Where's Grandpa?" David asked, dumping the bedding on the floor of his grandfather's room and beginning to strip the big bed.

"Gone to the post office to see if there's any mail," Nancy replied. "He'll be back soon." Then, suddenly remembering why David was not in school, she came to the door. "Did you get a job?" she asked softly.

"No," David began, "I —" But he got no further with his story, for just then the bell over the front door jangled. With a little sigh, Nancy laid down the clothing she was holding and went to wait on the customer who had come into the shop. She was wind-blown and panting for breath when she came back several minutes later.

"If a great tall man, with the longest legs you ever saw, and black hair and kind of twinkly eyes comes into the shop and wants a book, here is where it is," she announced, sticking a small gray book in the drawer of the cupboard. "He left it on the counter. I didn't see it till he'd been gone for a minute and then I chased him for a block, but I couldn't catch him."

"I hope he bought something," Mrs. Morgan said, appearing in the doorway with an armful of David's clothing. Then she spied her son, who was heaping sheets, blankets, quilts, and pillows into a pile on the floor. "Why, David Morgan, what on earth are you doing home at this hour? Is something wrong at school?"

"No," David said slowly. "I mean, yes. You see, Ma, I — " But once again David was interrupted, this time by a scuffling noise on the back steps, and Grandfather's voice declaring loudly, "It won't do you any good to struggle, my lad. I caught you right in the act."

Leaping over the piled-up bedding, David sprang to the door and yanked it open. There on the step stood Grandfather, his hand closed firmly on the collar of Jim's thin jacket. Half lifting, half pushing, the old man shoved the boy into the kitchen.

"Now, then," Grandfather said, still holding Jim fast and giving him a vigorous shake, "speak up, young fellow, and tell me what you were doing, sneaking out of our shed."

"He wasn't sneaking, Grandfather," David cried indignantly, grabbing his grandfather's arm. "He was looking for me! Let go of him! Please let go of him. That's Jim. He's my friend!"

chapter 3

Exciting Days

O F COURSE, as soon as Grandfather Morgan learned who Jim was and why he was coming from the shed, he released his hold on the boy's collar. Then, with Grandfather, Mother, and Nancy all listening attentively, David and Jim between them told the story of Jim's adventures and of their search for his father.

"So Jim doesn't know where to go now, and I told him you and Ma would help him," David said to his grandfather as the story drew to a close.

Grandfather nodded and started to ask a question, but Mrs. Morgan spoke first.

"What about your mother, Jim?" she asked. "Where is she?"

"I don't rightly know, ma'am," Jim replied, pulling

his jacket straight. "My pappy told me one day, 'way back, that once when Master Henry needed some money real bad he had to sell my mammy and my sister, too, along with some other folks. But I was only a little-bitty boy then and I don't remember them real good."

Nancy drew in her breath sharply. "Oh!" she exclaimed, "that's dreadful!" Then, rather shyly, she asked, "Did your — did your master ever beat you, Jim?"

"No, ma'am," Jim replied decidedly. "Master Henry was real good to all his people, an' so was Miss Lucy. If I hadn't wanted to be free so bad, and to be with my own pappy, I wouldn't never have left them."

Tears filled Jim's eyes for the second time that day, but he wiped them away hastily on the back of his hand. And Grandfather Morgan quickly changed the subject by asking to see the certificate of freedom which Jim's master had given him. Pushing aside the clothes which almost filled his big chair, Grandfather sat down in the space that remained and carefully read the rather grimy paper which Jim took from his pocket.

"It seems to be quite in order," he announced at last to the others, who were all watching him anxiously. "Jim, did your master ever tell you how important this paper is to you?"

Jim shook his head. "No, sir, he didn't say nothin' about it. He just give me the money my pappy sent, for me to ride on the railroad train, and told me how to get to Chicago and that I was free."

"Well, you're free just as long as you have this paper to prove it," Grandfather explained, folding the certificate and handing it back to Jim. "But don't you ever lose it. There's a law in this state — an evil, shameful law, but a law just the same — which says that all freed slaves who don't have papers like yours to prove that they are free shall be called runaways, and — "

"Land sakes, Grandfather Morgan, don't fret the poor boy with laws right now," Mother interrupted. "Nothing will happen to him as long as he's here with us, and I figure we can keep him here till he finds work or decides what he wants to do next. Now, do get up off those clothes. Mr. Snively may be back at any minute, and this place looks as if a cyclone had struck it."

Then she set Grandfather to carrying his clothing upstairs, asked Jim to help David take the big chair to the boys' room, and went with Nancy to make up the new boarder's bed. Next she sent David and Jim to clean out the back-yard shed.

"When it is all swept up, you can take a mattress and some bedding out there," she told them. "It's warm and snug, and Jim will be more comfortable there than here in the house, which is so crowded now that we fall all over one another."

So David and Jim went to work together to make the shed livable. They had just finished fixing a makeshift bed for Jim, and had returned to the house, when Peter and Robbie came running home from school. So amazed were the two younger children to find a strange colored boy in the kitchen, and to hear from Nancy about the new boarder, that they forgot to ask David why he hadn't been in school. And with one thing and another, it was not until late evening, after the supper dishes had been washed and put away, that the question came up.

Jim, who was worn out with his travels and grieving over the news of his father's death, had gone to bed in the shed, where he lay tossing uneasily in his unfamiliar surroundings.

Mrs. Morgan and Nancy, who had spent a very busy afternoon waiting on customers in the shop and making ready for Mr. Snively, were sitting close to the kitchen table, sewing by the light of the coal-oil lamp. Peter and Robbie were sprawled on the floor putting a puzzle together.

David's nose was buried in a book called *Strange Stories of a Detective,* which he had borrowed from a friend. Grandfather was looking over the *Chicago Press and Tribune.* And each one was wondering in the back of his mind what had happened to Mr. Snively, who had sent word by a messenger that he would not move in until the following day.

Suddenly Grandfather looked up from his newspaper and studied David with a perplexed frown.

"Shouldn't you be doing your lessons, my boy?" he asked.

David flushed and wriggled uncomfortably. "Well, no sir," he began. "The fact is — you see — " All at once he realized that everyone in the room was watching him curiously. So he straightened up in his chair and tried to sound very dignified. "As a matter of fact, Grandfather," he announced, "I've left that school forever. I'm not going back."

"Humph!" snorted Grandfather, peering at David over his spectacles, "I'll wager you've been in trouble again. Am I right?"

"Yes," admitted David, and forgetting to be dignified, he blurted out to the entire family the same story about his decision which he had told Nancy. "And so," he finished lamely, "I'm not going back to school at all. I'm going to get a job."

"And grow up a good-for-nothing ignoramus!" Grandfather spluttered, rattling his newspaper angrily. "Not if I know it. You'll march yourself back to that school tomorrow, young man, and —"

Mother dropped the pantaloons she was mending, into her lap. "Wait a minute, Grandfather Morgan," she said quietly. "I think perhaps David is right. Apparently he thinks he knows so much already that he doesn't need to study. And if he isn't working in school, he should certainly be working somewhere else. I heard you tell Jim before supper that you'd help him find a job tomorrow. I'd be glad if you'd help both boys get work together." She sent a meaningful glance in Grandfather's direction, and the old gentleman stroked his beard in silence for a moment.

"Well," he said at last, "I'll do it on one condition. David, I'll give you a letter tomorrow morning to my friend Mr. Page, who has just begun to build that new convention hall on the corner of Market and Lake

Streets. He's hiring all the help he can get, and even though you and Jim haven't any experience along those lines, I know he'll find work for both of you if I ask him to. In return for this, I'll expect you to study with me for two hours every evening. Will that be more agreeable to you than going back to the Dearborn School?"

"Yes sir," David replied meekly. He had been about to protest that he wasn't really interested in going on with any studying, and that what he wanted to do most was to work around boats. But something in his grandfather's voice and in the look in his mother's eyes stopped him.

So early the following morning David, with the note to Mr. Page clutched firmly in his hand, and Jim, with his certificate of freedom (which Grandfather had said he must always carry with him) safely pinned inside the pocket of his jacket, set off together in search of work. It was past five o'clock that afternoon when they returned dirty, tired, and hungry.

"We're building the biggest hall in this whole country," David announced happily to Nancy, as he soaped his hands at the kitchen sink, while Jim pumped water for him. "It'll be big enough to hold ten thousand people when it's done. One of the carpenters told me. Jingoes, Nance! There must be more than a hundred men working there."

"Are you a carpenter?" Peter asked, looking admiringly at his brother.

"Not yet," David admitted with a grin. "Jim and I

carry water to the men whenever they yell for it, and we fetch nails and help hoist lumber and do all sorts of things. It's hard work, isn't it, Jim?"

Jim nodded. "Never worked so hard in all my born days," he agreed. "But we get sixty cents a day all for ourselves, every day we works."

"And we're going to pay board to Ma, just the way Mr. Snively will — only not so much, of course — and Jim is going to live in our shed the rest of his life. We decided that on the way home, didn't we, Jim?"

"Unhuh," said Jim. "If your mammy and grand-pappy don't mind, I'd like it fine."

"We'll be glad to have you for as long as you want to stay, Jim," Mrs. Morgan declared. Grandfather nodded his head in agreement. So the matter was arranged to the satisfaction of all.

And now, every day, David and Jim went off to work together. There were mornings, once in a while, when David crawled out of bed sleepily, thought of the hard work which lay ahead, and almost wished that he were back in school. But on the whole he found it exciting to watch the big hall slowly taking shape, and to be working with grown men.

As for Jim, the fact that he was his own master and earning his own money made him feel so fine that no work would have seemed too difficult. Every evening he helped David with his chores around the house and shop, and the two boys soon became fast friends.

One night when David was working at the kitchen

table on a spelling lesson which Grandfather had set for him, Jim hung over the other boy's chair, watching intently as he copied the words. And the next day he asked Mrs. Morgan if he might borrow one of Robbie's easy reading books.

"We never did let on to Master Henry, 'cause he was plumb set against breakin' the law and lettin' his colored folks have any schoolin', especially after my pappy ran away, but Miss Lucy, she taught me to write my name and to read some," he explained. "I just don't want my eyes to forget what the words look like, 'cause someday I aims to get myself some real book learnin'."

"And what will you do with book learning, Jim?" Mrs. Morgan asked, handing the boy an old reader of Robbie's.

Jim shrugged his shoulders. "I don't know yet, ma'am," he answered with a slow grin. "I just know I got a hankerin' to learn."

And learn he did, asking so many questions about words and their meanings that Grandfather soon began to set lessons for him, too, teaching him to spell and write and figure.

Mr. Snively, who had moved in the day after Jim's arrival, seemed curious about the boy from the moment he saw him, and asked all manner of things about him. He wanted to know Jim's full name, where he had come from, who his master had been, and why he was in Chicago. Even after Grandfather had explained all about Jim's father and the certificate of freedom, David caught the new boarder, once or twice, looking at Jim with a strange expression on his face.

"Like Inky watching a bird," David thought. But as the family became more accustomed to having Mr. Snively around, the boy forgot all about this strange behavior. And he laughed at Nancy one day, when she insisted that she still disliked the man who was living in her grandfather's room.

It was on a Sunday early in May. Jim had gone, as usual, to spend the day with the family of a colored waiter who had been a friend of his father's. The Morgans were on their way to church, and Nancy and David, who were walking behind the others, were talking about Mr. Snively.

"I don't care if he did give Peter a baseball bat for his birthday and get us all ice cream," Nancy declared, hanging onto her bonnet as a gust of wind swept down the street. "There's something about that Mr. Snively that I just don't like."

"Jim doesn't like him either," David remarked. "I wonder why."

"Well, for one thing," Nancy said, "he's always asking prying questions. I heard him ask Jim yesterday the names of his friends and where they live. Why should he want to know? And for another thing, he's too mysterious about himself. Every time Grandfather starts to ask him what work he is doing, old Snively changes the subject. I'd like to know what he does all day and where he goes when he stays away from our house two and three days at a time."

David chuckled. "That's just like a girl!" he teased. "Fretting because a man asks too many questions, and then wanting to know all about his business."

Nancy's face flushed. "Just the same, Davy," she insisted, "I don't like him, and I think he's up to something crooked."

With a grin, David changed the subject, never dreaming that the day would come when he would remember this conversation sadly and wish that he had listened more attentively to his sister.

Things were going well now with the Morgan family. Business was good in the little shop. With Mr. Snively, David, and Jim all paying board, Mrs. Morgan was no longer so worried about money. Grandfather, who was busy writing his book on early days in Chicago, was getting on well with his work. Peter and Robbie were doing nicely in school. Nancy, who had a high, sweet voice, had been invited, to her great delight, to join a singing class which met in the neighborhood. And David had pleased both his mother and grandfather by working so hard at his job that he had been made a helper to one of the carpenters.

Already the great convention hall which David and Jim were helping to build was nearing completion. Mother said that to hear the boys talk about it one would almost think that it belonged just to them.

"It's called the Wigwam, and when it's finished Jim and I'll take you to see it," David told his brothers one evening, as he and Jim sat on the back steps with them, cracking nuts for Nancy to use in her baking.

"Is it going to have Indians in it?" Peter asked hopefully.

"Nope — not Indians, just Republicans," David said, popping a nut kernel into his mouth. "Grandpa says they're coming here from all over the country pretty soon, to choose the man they want to run for President next time Election Day comes around." He spat out a piece of shell. "I know who I'd choose," he added thoughtfully.

"Who?" asked Jim, cracking two walnuts together in his strong brown hands. "Your grandpa?"

David shook his head. "He's too old," he said. "I'd choose the man Grandpa wants for President, though. The one he's always talking about and reading about in the newspapers — that Mr. Lincoln. I think he must be a nice man, Jim."

"Master Henry didn't think so," Jim said, reaching for a nutpick. "I done heard him talk plenty about that Mr. Lincoln before I left Kentucky. Once it near scalded me to death, his talkin' did."

"How?" asked Peter, looking wide-eyed at Jim.

Jim chuckled. "Oh, I was carrying a big tureen full of soup to the dinner table one day, and Master Henry, he was talkin' real mad, like he did sometimes, poundin' his fist on the table and makin' the dishes jump. And just as I come up close he yells at Miss Lucy something about Mr. Lincoln is a blasted fool, always stirrin' up trouble by tellin' folks slavery is wicked. And then his hand shot out in the air, and the next thing I knew I was hot soup all over and jumping up and down worse than the dishes on the table."

"Poor Jim! Did you get burned badly?" Robbie asked.

"Miss Lucy had to smear sweet oil on my hands and legs for more than a week," Jim replied rather proudly, raising his voice as a horsecar rattled past the house.

It was just at that instant that Nancy stepped to the kitchen door.

"Lesson time, Dave," she said. "Grandpa is waiting for you and Jim."

So, brushing the broken nutshells from their pantaloons, the two older boys went inside the house. Robbie and Peter followed them almost immediately, each carrying a plate of nut meats. And for the time being both the Wigwam and Mr. Abraham Lincoln were forgotten.

But they were not forgotten for long. It was the very next afternoon that Grandfather brought home from the post office a letter for Mrs. Morgan. He took it to her in the shop, where she had just finished wrapping up a pound of rock candy for a fat old lady. As soon as the customer had paid for her purchase, put her change carefully in her purse, and departed, Mrs. Morgan tore open the envelope. Glancing hastily at the note it contained, she passed it to Nancy with a smile. Nancy read it through more slowly.

"Can we go?" she asked her mother eagerly.

"If Grandfather will tend shop for us," Mrs. Morgan replied.

As soon as Grandfather had read the note he readily agreed to take care of the shop. And that night when David and Jim came home from work, Nancy's eyes were dancing as she met them at the door.

"You aren't the only ones in this family to work on that Wigwam you talk so much about, Davy," she teased. "You and Jim only work on the outside. Mother and I are going to help trim the inside."

"How does that happen?" David asked, unbelievingly.

Nancy tossed her head. "Oh, we had a letter from Mrs. Rankin today, asking us to a sewing bee to help make draperies and banners and things," she said. "And all the ladies who help with the decorations will have tickets to the convention."

"Humph!" said David scornfully. "You're not a lady yet, and anyway who wants to go to an old convention?"

Nevertheless, as the time for the Republican Convention drew near, David became more and more eager to go. Indeed, it seemed as though all the people in Chicago, as well as thousands of men and women from other parts of the country, were hoping to get into the Wigwam, where the delegates from the various states in the Union would select the Republican candidate for the office of President of the United States.

By the middle of May so many visitors had come flocking to Chicago that every hotel and boarding-house in the city was full. Again and again some member of the Morgan family went to the door of their little home to turn away people who came seeking a room to rent, or a bed to sleep in, until after the Convention was over.

New customers poured into the shop in such numbers that Mrs. Morgan could not begin to fill their needs. And David and Jim, whose work on the Wigwam was ended, were kept busy from morning till night, running errands and helping in the kitchen.

Never before had the city been so gay. Flags flew from nearly every building. Houses, stores, and offices were festooned with bunting of red, white, and blue. From sunup till long past sundown visitors crowded the streets. They peered into shop windows, craned their necks to watch the parades which seemed to spring up from nowhere, kept step to the lively music of the bands, and stopped on street corners to argue about which man would be nominated by the Republican Party.

Some were all for a man named Seward, from New York State. Others hoped to see a Mr. Chase from Ohio nominated. Still others declared that either Edward Bates from Missouri or Simon Cameron of Pennsylvania would be a fine candidate. But those people who lived in Chicago, and indeed most of the people in the state of Illinois, had only one name in their minds.

"We want a man from our own part of the country," they said to everyone who would listen. "A strong man who isn't afraid to say what he thinks. A man who hates slavery and will work to keep it from spread-

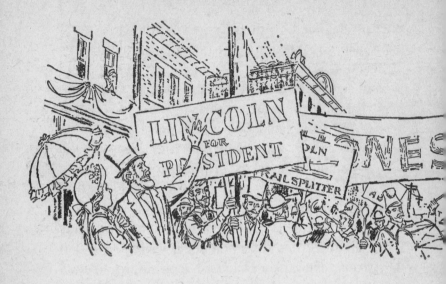

ing any farther in this land. A man we can trust. We want Abe Lincoln. Honest old Abe."

And everywhere throughout the city — on buildings, on omnibuses, on banners which stretched high overhead across the streets, on badges worn on thousands of coats — were pictures of Abraham Lincoln.

Those pictures bothered Nancy. Every time she saw one, whether it was the huge crayon portrait which hung in the Wigwam on the evenings she helped trim the hall with banners and garlands of evergreen, or whether it was one of the smaller pictures on the badges Grandfather and the boys were wearing, she was troubled by something she felt she ought to remember — and couldn't.

And then, early one morning when she was standing in front of the bedroom mirror, braiding her hair

and wishing there were some way to get rid of the freckle on the end of her nose, she knew suddenly what it was.

"That's it! That's the man!" she exclaimed aloud. Without giving her startled mother time to ask what she was talking about, she picked up her long, full skirt, ran down the stairs, and began to rummage in the drawer of the kitchen cupboard.

Grandfather turned from the sink, his face dripping and covered with soapsuds.

"What in thunder are you looking for, Nance?" he asked, as Nancy tumbled a pile of dish towels, a tea strainer, and a ball of string to the floor in her haste.

"Abraham Lincoln!" Nancy said quickly. "He was here, Grandpa, right in our very own shop. I remember now — he left —"

She stopped, felt deeper in the drawer, and pulled out the small gray book which she had tucked away and forgotten many weeks earlier.

"Here it is!" she cried triumphantly. "It's his book! I know it is!"

"That hardly seems likely," Grandfather said, plunging his face into a basin full of water and reaching blindly for a towel. "See if there's a name in it."

"There is," Nancy announced happily. "Right on the front page — A. Lincoln. Just think, Grandfather, that man has his picture all over Chicago, and maybe someday he'll be President of the whole country — only Mr. Snively says a man named Douglas is going to be — and he bought some candy from me right in our very own shop." She sighed, and stroked the book lovingly. "He said it was for his little boys. I wish I could remember what kind he bought."

Grandfather laughed. "You chatter on like a magpie, Nance!" he exclaimed. Then, taking the book from Nancy, he looked through several pages. "It's a handy little dictionary," he declared. "Just the right size to fit into a pocket. I'll wager Mr. Lincoln's missed it."

"What are you going to do with it?" Nancy asked, as the old man turned to leave the room with the book in his hands.

"Put it away in my desk," Grandfather replied over his shoulder. "As soon as all this excitement about the convention is over, I'll wrap it up and mail it to him."

But months were to pass and many exciting things were to happen before that small gray dictionary, with the name "A. Lincoln" written carefully on its front page, was to reach its rightful owner.

chapter 4

Good News—and Trouble

IT SEEMED to Robbie that he had been standing in the crowd which had gathered in front of the Wigwam on the morning of Friday, May 18, for at least a week. His legs ached. One foot had a cramp in it. People were constantly bumping against him, shoving him around, and stepping on his toes.

His ears rang with the blaring of bands and the noise made by excited men and women who shouted and cheered wildly every once in a while about something he didn't understand. And he couldn't see a thing, when he looked ahead, but the gray shawl of a fat woman who had just poked him in the nose with her elbow.

Robbie wished that he had been able to earn a

ticket into the Wigwam as Nancy had, and could be sitting beside Grandfather, as she probably was that very minute. He wished he were as tall as David or Jim, who were standing on either side of him and were able to see all that was going on. He almost wished he were Peter, who had awakened that morning with red eyes and such a sniffly cold that Mother had kept him home in bed and had stayed at home to take care of him. Shifting his weight from one foot to the other, he tugged at David's jacket.

"How much longer do we have to wait, Davy?" he asked, yelling to make himself heard above the voices of the jostling, pushing crowd. "I'm kind of tired. Isn't it ever going to end?"

David looked down at his younger brother, smiled and opened his mouth to reply. But at that very instant a roar of voices and a burst of applause, like a roll of thunder, came through the open windows of the Wigwam.

"Hooray!" shouted an old man standing next to David. "The delegates have voted! By cracky! They've voted at last."

"Seward's leading!" another man yelled, leaning out of a Wigwam window and waving his hat at the people below him. "Seward's ahead! Seward will win! Seward's ahead!"

"Seward!"

" 'Ray for Seward!"

"Seward for President!"

"Seward! Seward! Seward!" screamed hundreds of

voices in the crowd in the street.

But from hundreds of other throats there were groans — and cries of "Lincoln!"

"Give us Lincoln!"

"We want Lincoln!"

"Three cheers for old Abe!"

Inside the Wigwam, Nancy peered down from the balcony where she was sitting squeezed in tightly between Grandfather and a man she did not know. The crowd below her was in a turmoil. Men were parading up and down the aisles, carrying placards on which were printed the names of the states from which they had come, and pictures of their candidates.

Bands were blaring. People were yelling excitedly at one another. On the long platform at the front of the hall, important-looking gentlemen in tall hats, tightly fitting pantaloons, and long frock coats were hurrying about, talking together, nodding their heads, shaking their heads, whispering behind their hands, and shouting questions to other men on the floor below.

"What are they all doing?" Nancy cried excitedly to Grandfather, who was thumping his cane on the floor and yelling Lincoln's name at the top of his lungs. "What are they all doing? I thought Mr. Seward won. He had more votes than Mr. Lincoln."

"Not enough more!" Grandfather shouted. "Not a majority! The delegates will have to vote again."

And again the delegates cast their ballots. Again, when the votes were counted, Mr. Seward was in the lead.

"But only by three and a half votes, by jingoes!" Grandfather cried, standing up in his excitement and pulling Nancy up beside him. "Only three and a half! They'll have to vote once more."

As the delegates cast their ballots for the third time, the cheering and shouting in the great hall died down. The talking stopped. Men sat tensely, or stood almost without moving while the third lot of votes was counted. Except for the clicking of the telegraph, which was sending news of the Republican Convention out over the country, there was hardly a sound in the Wigwam.

And then, to the front of the platform stepped the chairman of the convention.

"Ladies and gentlemen!" he cried. "Abraham Lincoln of Illinois is selected as your candidate for President of the United States."

There was a breathless moment of silence. Then such a roar of voices filled the air that the Wigwam seemed to rock back and forth. Men and women leaped up and down — screaming, waving handkerchiefs and flags, tossing hats and canes and umbrellas into the air, laughing, pounding their feet, hugging one another, weeping with happiness.

"Hallelujah!" shouted a man on the platform. "Hallelujah! Abe Lincoln is nominated!"

A cannon on the roof of the Wigwam boomed to let the city know the glad news, and the people in the street let out a mighty yell. From the Tremont House, five blocks away, a hundred guns blazed.

Riverboat whistles set up a squealing. Locomotive whistles tooted. Factory bells jangled. Chimes in church steeples pealed. Bands everywhere began to play. And through all the tumult the name of Lincoln was heard again and again and again, as the thousands of shouting men and women in the streets around the Wigwam swayed back and forth, pushing and jostling against one another in their excitement.

A tall man in the crowd banged his hat down on David's head in his joy. David winced.

"We'd better get out of here," he cried, grabbing Jim by the arm. Then he looked startled. "Hey!" he exclaimed, "where's Robbie?"

"Don't know!" Jim replied. "I thought he was standing on the other side of you."

"I thought you had him beside you," David said, and he began to call "Robbie! Robbie!" and to push his way through the crowd, looking here and there for his brother.

Jim followed close behind him. "We'll never find him this way," he shouted after several minutes of searching. "Maybe he just got tired and went on home."

"Maybe," David cried over his shoulder. "I'm going home to find out."

With Jim at his heels, he worked his way to the edge of the crowd, crossed a vacant lot, ran down an alley, and started east along Randolph Street, toward State Street, at a dogtrot.

Both boys were breathless when they reached home

and burst into the kitchen. Mother, who had put a sign on the shop door saying "Closed until Monday Afternoon," was sitting near the window, reading.

"Sh!" she said, putting a warning finger to her lips. "Peter's asleep. Mr. Lincoln was nominated, wasn't he? I could tell by the noise."

David nodded. "Did Robbie come home?" he asked.

"Come home?" Mother repeated in surprise. "What do you mean? He was with you, and you promised to watch him. What's happened to him?"

"I don't know," David replied, looking very crest-fallen. And he explained to his mother how he and Jim had discovered that Robbie was missing.

Mrs. Morgan was worried. "How long do you think he's been gone?" she asked.

"Well," David said slowly, pulling thoughtfully at his upper lip, "it must have been — jingoes, Ma, it must have been more than an hour ago that I noticed him last. It's been kind of exciting over there with all the yelling and —"

Mrs. Morgan nodded. "I know," she said. "Robbie probably just grew tired of standing still and wandered off, looking for something more interesting to do. His head's so full of boats these days, I think the chances are that he's gone to the lake."

"Shall we go and look for him?" David asked.

"Yes," replied Mother. "If he's not there, then search the river docks. And be sure you come straight back with him if you find him. I'll be uneasy in my mind until he's safely home."

"We'll hurry," David and Jim promised together, and they set off for the long, narrow beach east of Michigan Avenue, where they had met for the first time many weeks earlier and where the children from the neighboring streets often went to play.

The day was warm for mid-May, and there were a number of people strolling along the water's edge, or standing about discussing the convention and exclaiming over the noisy celebration which was still going on all over the city. An old man sitting on an overturned box was combing out the shaggy hair of a big brown and white dog. Two boys were patching the bottom of a leaky sailboat, and several little girls were building a castle in the sand. But nowhere was there any sign of Robbie.

David, who was beginning to feel really alarmed about his small brother's disappearance, went up to the little girls and spoke to one of them.

"Hello, Gretchen," he said. "Have you seen Robbie anywhere around?"

The child called Gretchen looked up at David and nodded her head solemnly, her short yellow pigtails bobbing up and down.

"Where is he?" asked David quickly. "My mother wants him."

"Out there," Gretchen said, pointing to the water with a stubby finger. "He took my father's rowboat."

"He did!" exclaimed David, swinging around to look out over the water. "Who told him he could do that?"

"Me," Gretchen said, bending over to build up a wall of sand which had crumbled. "My father's rich. He has two boats. He wouldn't care."

Jim's eyes, too, were scanning the lagoon which lay between the beach and the railroad trestle.

"There's five rowboats out there and a sailboat, and Robbie ain't in any of 'em," he announced. "You ain't foolin' us, is you, Gretchen?"

"Of course she isn't," piped up one of the other little girls, staring curiously at Jim. "Robbie had some string and a hook in his pocket, and he's gone fishing out on the lake."

David whistled under his breath. "Crazy little fool!" he exclaimed anxiously. "He can't swim a stroke. Grandpa will whip him, sure as shooting, if he finds this out."

He turned to Jim. "We'll have to go out on the breakwater and holler at him to come in," he said. And he started up the beach toward a place some distance away, where it was possible to cross the tracks to the wall of piling and rocks which protected the railroad trestle from the waters of Lake Michigan. Jim followed him.

Climbing over the railroad tracks, the boys reached the breakwater. The great lake, stretching as far as the eye could see, was blue and sparkling in the bright spring sunshine. There was almost no wind — hardly enough to fill the sails of several small boats which were moving slowly across the water. A big four-masted schooner, anchored some distance off shore, seemed almost motionless, and a gray gull was floating in the air without a wing flap.

"Good thing it's a calm day," David remarked. "Robbie'd never be able to manage a boat here if the lake wasn't as still as a millpond."

He shaded his eyes and looked along the breakwater to a spot where he knew it was possible for boats to pass between the pilings from the lagoon to the lake.

But Jim had already spied Robbie. "There he is," he announced, pointing to a child in a rowboat which floated quietly on the water several hundred yards to the south, and only a little way from the breakwater. "He seems to be just lettin' the boat drift wherever it wants to."

David made a trumpet of his hands. "Hey, Robbie," he shouted, "you get back to the shore as fast as you can."

But the small boy, who was dangling a string from the stern of the boat, did not even look up.

"He can't hear you," Jim said. "Wait till we get nearer." And he began to scramble along the breakwater as fast as he could.

"Robbie," David yelled again as soon as he and Jim were within hailing distance. "Robbie, Ma wants you. You come in right away."

This time Robbie looked around with a guilty grin.

"All right, Davy," he called. "I'm coming. Just a minute." Pulling in his string, he stood up and started to step to the rowing seat in the center of the boat.

"Watch out!" David cried. "Keep to the middle."

But his warning came too late. All at once the boat tipped. Robbie lost his balance, waved his arms in the air, and pitched overboard with a great splash.

"Lawsy!" exclaimed Jim under his breath.

"Hang onto the boat," David yelled, as Robbie's head appeared above the surface of the water. "We're coming!"

By this time both David and Jim were scrambling down the rocks, slipping and sliding in their haste to reach the water.

Choking, spluttering, and thoroughly frightened, Robbie was thrashing about wildly in the chilly lake, while the boat was slowly drifting farther and farther away from him.

"Davy!" he yelled feebly. "Davy! Help!"

"We're coming. Don't get scared!" Jim called, as the two boys plunged into the water without even stopping to remove their jackets.

Fortunately they were both strong swimmers, and even though they were weighed down with clothing, they reached Robbie quickly. Swimming up behind the frightened child, Jim grabbed him by the collar.

"Stop wavin' your arms like that," he gasped, "or I'll duck you. I've got you. You're all right now." Then, as he saw David approaching Robbie from the front, he warned, "Keep away, Dave. He might grab you 'round the neck. I've got hold of him. Get the rowboat."

Treading water, Jim managed somehow to keep

Robbie's head above the surface until David had pushed the rowboat close enough for the little boy to hang onto it. With great effort because of his water-soaked boots, David clambered into the boat. He pulled, Jim pushed, and between them they soon had Robbie over the side.

The child lay huddled in a heap on the bottom of the boat for a minute, half crying and gasping for breath. Then he struggled to a sitting position and peered down at Jim, who was resting in the water with one brown hand on the gunwale.

"Are you all right, Jim?" he asked tearfully.

Jim drew a deep breath. "Reckon so," he said. "Move over so's I can get in."

Puffing and panting, he hoisted himself at last into the rowboat. For several minutes no one spoke. Then David laughed weakly.

"You t-t-two l-look like d-d-drowned rats," he stammered, trying to keep his teeth from chattering.

Jim shivered. "I f-feel l-l-like one," he said. "L-let's get home as f-f-fast as we c-can."

David nodded, picked up the oars, which by great good luck were still in the boat, and started to row toward the lagoon.

Gretchen and her little friends had completed their castle and left the beach, so the boys attracted no attention as they climbed out of the boat, pulled it up on the sand, and hurried off toward home. They were a sorry sight as they made their way hastily through the streets, with their hair plastered flat to their heads, their clothing dripping with water, and their lips blue with cold. Several people smiled sympathetically as they passed by, and old Mr. Ziegler, who kept the butcher store on State Street a block away from the Morgans' house, called out to ask jokingly why they had gone swimming so early in the season.

At this, Robbie, who was dreading the punishment he thought was in store for him, began to whimper again. He was crying loudly by the time David and Jim hurried him up the back steps and into the kitchen, and the noise brought Mrs. Morgan, who had just gone upstairs in answer to a cry from Peter, flying back again.

"Merciful heavens!" she cried, dropping to her knees on the floor before Robbie and feeling him all over. "Are you hurt? Where have you been? Stop howling like that and tell me what's the matter."

"H-h-he's all right," David stammered. "He just went f-fishing and f-fell in the l-l-lake, and w-we —"

"Never mind," Mrs. Morgan interrupted. "Don't stop to tell me now, Dave. You and Jim get out of those wet clothes and into dry ones as fast as you can, or I'll have you all sick in bed like Peter."

She pulled off Robbie's jacket and began to unbutton his blouse. David turned obediently and went upstairs in search of dry clothing. But Jim stood as if rooted to the spot. His mouth dropped open and his eyes filled with terror. Fumbling in his jacket pocket, he fished out a soggy mess of white pulp.

"My freedom paper!" he moaned. "My freedom paper!"

With shaking fingers he attempted to unfold his certificate of freedom. But the paper came apart in his hands, and the words which had once announced that he was no longer a slave were blurred beyond recognition.

"It's done ruined!" he cried sadly. "It's ruined for fair. It ain't no good to me no more at all." And, choking back a sob, he turned and ran out of the kitchen.

Mrs. Morgan sighed. "It looks as if we were in for a run of trouble," she said, half to herself and half to Robbie, as she stripped him of his pantaloons. "Now you take off your boots and your underclothes, and get yourself upstairs and into my bed as fast as you can. Don't go near Peter. I think he has the measles. I'm going out to speak to Jim."

Giving Robbie a little push toward the stairs, she went out to the shed and knocked on the door. In answer to Jim's muffled "Come in," she stepped inside, to find the boy still in his wet clothes, sitting on the edge of the bed, a picture of despair.

"I'm a slave again, Mrs. Morgan," Jim said dully, his brown eyes clouded with tears. "Mr. Morgan done tole me often what would happen if I lost my paper. I'm nothin' but a slave again. I ain't free no more."

"Nonsense, Jim," Mrs. Morgan exclaimed, trying to sound more cheerful about Jim's predicament than she felt. "Just remember not to say anything to anyone about what's happened, and we'll send a letter immediately to your Master Henry, explaining the matter to him and asking him to make out another certificate for you."

"Can you do that, ma'am?" Jim asked, and his face brightened.

"I'll write the letter myself," Mrs. Morgan promised. Then she hurried back to the house to warn David, Robbie, and Peter that they must be very careful not to speak of Jim's loss to anyone except Nancy and Grandfather.

That night before she went to bed she wrote the promised letter to Mr. Henry Taylor of Higginsville, Kentucky. And early the following morning Grandfather carried it to the post office and sent it on its way.

chapter 5

More Trouble

NANCY LOVED her grandfather dearly, but there were times when it seemed to her that he did the most exasperating things. Why, she wondered, as she handed Mr. Ziegler thirty cents for three pounds of his best beefsteak, why had Grandfather chosen today of all days to invite Mr. Snively to supper?

Peter was spending his second day in bed, and in spite of the fact that no spots had appeared, his head was hot and his eyes were redder than ever. Robbie was in bed, too, sniffling and sneezing. Although David and Jim were apparently none the worse for their swim of the day before, poor Jim was so frightened and unhappy over the loss of his certificate of freedom that he had stayed in the shed all day. Even with the shop closed, it had been a difficult day for everyone — hardly the time to invite anyone for a meal.

"Especially that man!" Nancy thought, wrinkling her nose in disgust, for she still had an uncomfortable feeling, which she could not explain even to herself, whenever Mr. Snively was around.

Tucking her package of meat under her arm, she darted across Monroe Street, which was still gay with flags, banners, and streamers, and hurried home to lay the table with the best linen cloth and to help her mother get supper.

In spite of the fact that it was a last-minute affair, the meal was delicious. Mother and Nancy were so busy waiting on the table and running upstairs to take care of Peter and Robbie that they did not have much time to enjoy it. But Mr. Snively, Grandfather, and David tucked away beefsteak, fried potatoes, hot rolls and butter, coffee, and freshly baked apple pie with great relish. Then Grandfather wiped his beard carefully on his napkin, pushed his chair back from the table, and crossed one knee over the other.

"Yes, Mr. Snively," he said, continuing a conversation he had begun earlier, "I came to Chicago 'way back in 1830. Fort Dearborn was standing then, and there wasn't much of anything else here. Just some wigwams and a few log huts. No people but Indians and fur trappers. And look at the city today, Mr. Snively! One of the finest in the land and strong enough to have a hand in nominating the next President of the United States."

Mr. Snively pried with his finger at a piece of meat, which had lodged between two front teeth, and shook his head.

"That man Lincoln won't never be President, Mr. Morgan," he declared. "Don't you fool yourself. Folks in the South ain't ever going to let a man who's so set against slavery get elected.

"No sir, they're all talking about sending Stephen Douglas to the White House, 'cause he's all for slavery. Says right out, he does, that slaves are property like horses or cows and that a man's got a right to take property anywhere he's a mind to. I don't take sides, of course, one way or the order, but that seems reasonable to me. Don't it to you?"

Grandfather flushed angrily and opened his mouth to reply. But Mrs. Morgan, who realized that the two men might be starting a long and perhaps an unpleasant argument, laid her napkin on the table at that moment and stood up.

"If you will all excuse me, I will carry some supper to Jim. The poor boy has hardly eaten a thing all day," she said. And taking a plate full of warm food from the stove, she left the room. It was just then that Grandfather also excused himself and went upstairs in answer to a call from Robbie. Nancy and David were left alone in the kitchen with Mr. Snively.

"What's wrong with Jim today?" Mr. Snively asked, looking from one to the other. "Is he sick, too?"

Nancy shook her head. "Not really," she said. "Jim's just worried because his free — " She broke off suddenly, coughed, and leaning down, ducked her head under the table, pretending to look on the floor for her napkin. But David, without stopping to think what he was doing, hurried to finish her sentence.

"His freedom paper was spoiled yesterday, you see, when he swam out in the lake after Robbie," he explained.

"Spoiled, eh!" repeated Mr. Snively, tipping back in his chair and linking his pudgy hands over his stomach. "Hmm! That's a shame! Yes, that's a real shame. It's sad business for Jim, and it puts you folks in a mighty mean spot, too, don't it?"

"No-o-o," David said doubtfully, his face growing red as he realized suddenly what he had done. "I don't see why it should."

"Then, my boy," remarked Mr. Snively, twirling his thumbs and staring at a spot on the ceiling, "you don't know the law. As I recollect it, the law reads that anyone in this state caught giving shelter to a Negro who don't have papers to prove that he's free shall be fined five hundred dollars. Half of that tidy little sum gits paid to the county where the Negro is staying and the other half goes to the person who reports the matter to the police."

It seemed to Nancy that there was almost a joyful note in Mr. Snively's voice as he finished. Trying to hide the feeling of dismay which swept over her, she said lightly, "Oh well, Jim will have a new certificate pretty soon. Mother has written a letter about it already."

"And no one outside the family knows what's happened, anyway," David added quickly. "That is, no one but you, and you'd never report us because you're our friend."

Mr. Snively laughed abruptly. "Sure, I'm your friend," he declared. "One of the best you've ever had, too, and I give you my word I'll not mention this matter to anyone who'd get you in trouble. Now, let's all three forget that you two have let the secret slip out and say no more about it, shall we?"

Nancy and David nodded their heads gratefully, and no further mention of Jim's certificate of freedom was made by anyone that evening.

The next day was Sunday. Both Robbie and Peter woke up with sore throats and fever, and they were as cross as two sticks. Jim did not go as usual to visit his friends, the Jenkins family, but stayed home all day. No one went to church, and the only person who left the house was Mr. Snively. He went out early in the morning and did not come back until long after dark.

By the time he returned, Nancy and Grandfather had gone up to bed, and David, who had been coughing and sneezing all day, was almost asleep on his cot in the corner of the kitchen. Mother was seated at the table, just finishing a letter to her sister Hattie, who lived in Springfield, Illinois. She laid down her pen, looked up, and nodded a greeting as Mr. Snively came in.

After saying "Good evening," that gentleman crossed

the room and handed Mrs. Morgan his back-door key. Then, speaking in a low voice so that he would not disturb David, he announced that he would not need his room after that night, since he was planning to depart from Chicago the following day.

"My work in your fair city is done up brown, ma'am," he said. "There ain't no reason for me to linger on another day. You tell Mr. Morgan and the children good-by for me, 'cause I'll be leaving early in the morning — long before they or anyone else is up."

David, who had been listening with one ear to the conversation, rolled over in bed on hearing this and propped himself up on his elbow.

"Where are you going, Mr. Snively?" he asked.

"Just pushin' on a mite farther west tomorrow," Mr. Snively replied, twirling his hat in his hands. "Can't tell right now where I'll land, though. Here, there, everywhere — that's Adelbert Snively. Somehow I don't seem to be able to stay in any one place very long, without getting a hankering to move on."

He turned to Mrs. Morgan. "Well, ma'am," he continued, "I'll say good-by to you now and get to my room and pack my duds."

Mrs. Morgan stood up. "You must tell me what time you're leaving, and I'll see that you get some breakfast before you go," she said.

"No, indeedy! I wouldn't think of puttin' you to all that trouble, ma'am," Mr. Snively exclaimed emphatically. "A friend of mine who came to see the convention is drivin' out of town tomorrow, and he'll stop by in his wagon before daylight to pick me up. We'll eat breakfast somewhere along the way. I'll go out real quiet like, so's I won't disturb anybody."

He looked at David. "And you, Davy," he added, "if you hear me creeping through the kitchen in the dark, don't you pay any heed at all. Just go right back to sleep like a good lad, will you?"

Smothering a yawn, David nodded, said good-by sleepily, and lay down. After a few more words with Mrs. Morgan, Mr. Snively disappeared into his room. Mrs. Morgan lighted a candle, blew out the lamp, and went quietly upstairs. Except for a thin ray of light coming through the crack under Mr. Snively's door, the kitchen was left in darkness.

Pulling the covers up under his chin, David shut his eyes and drifted off to sleep. But he did not sleep well. Perhaps it was because Mr. Snively was moving about in the next room. Perhaps it was because of a feeling of uneasiness which had hung over him ever since he and Nancy had given away Jim's secret. Perhaps it was just because he had eaten too many doughnuts for supper, in spite of the fact that his head ached.

At any rate, he turned and tossed and had one bad dream after another all night. The last and most vivid dream was about Jim. David dreamed that he and Jim were standing together on a slippery rock out in the middle of the lake.

Suddenly a great black water snake, with a beard like Grandfather's and big pop eyes, reared out of the water, slithered up one side of the rock and down the other, wrapping his slimy tail around Jim's legs and pulling him along into the lake. Jim yelled, "Help, David! Help!" as he disappeared beneath the surface of the water. But when David plunged into the lake after his friend, he found himself in a huge hall like the Wigwam, chasing a blue rabbit and crying, "Wait! I'm coming! I'm coming!"

It was this dream that woke up David with a start. Sitting bolt upright in bed, he stared around the kitchen. The thin streak of light which had come from the crack under Mr. Snively's door was there no longer, and the door itself was open. Through the kitchen window came the muffled sound of a man's voice saying, "Easy does it. Here we go."

Then there was a thud as though something heavy had been thrown to a wooden floor. Next another voice, which David knew was Mr. Snively's, urged, "Hurry, Frank. Shake a leg!"

A moment of complete silence followed this remark, and then came the sound of horses' hoofs and wagon wheels rolling away down the cobblestone street.

"Well," David thought sleepily, "he's gone. Wonder why he was in such a hurry?" And, sinking back on his pillow, he dropped off to sleep again just as the first rooster crowed to welcome the dawn, and the robins nesting in the lilac bush near the kitchen door began their morning song.

He did not waken until Nancy came down in her red flannel wrapper, shook him by the shoulder, and told him it was time to get up.

"The sun's shining and Peter is feeling a little better, and that horrid old frog is gone and I'm so happy I could sing," she announced, as she started back to her room to braid her hair and finish dressing.

David did not reply. Rubbing his eyes and stretching, he swung his legs over the edge of the bed and reached for his clothes. It did not take him long to put them on and to splash his face with cold water from the pump in the kitchen sink. Then, combing his hair with his fingers, he went outside to arouse Jim, who was a heavy sleeper and seldom wakened until David pounded on the door of the shed. This time, as frequently happened, there was no answer to David's knock.

"Hey, Jim, you lazybones, wake up," David cried, and, pushing open the door, he stepped into the shed.

Then he stared about him in surprise. Jim's bed was empty, the covers thrown aside. His clothing, which he usually folded neatly and laid on the bench near the door, was gone. In its place was a piece of paper, torn from the copybook which Grandfather had given Jim to use for his spelling lessons.

There were a few words scrawled on the paper, and a stick of wood had been laid across it so that it would not blow away. Picking up the paper, David read the penciled message once and then again, as though he could not believe what he saw.

Then, wheeling around suddenly, he rushed into the house and started for the stairs, colliding in the narrow hallway with Grandfather, who was on his way to the kitchen.

"Lord save us, lad!" the old gentleman spluttered. "A body'd think you were running to a fire. Can't you see where —"

David interrupted him. "Grandpa!" he cried forlornly. "Look at this. Jim's gone!" And he thrust into his grandfather's hand the message he had found in the shed. It was short and simple, and this is what it said:

"Gone to Canada. Good-by. Jim."

chapter 6

A Mysterious Visitor

I N SPITE OF the message found in the shed, no one in the Morgan family, except perhaps Peter and Robbie, really believed for more than a minute or so that Jim was on his way north.

Although they did not mention it at once, David and Nancy both remembered with sinking hearts the conversation which had occurred at the supper table two evenings earlier. Mother announced, immediately after hearing the contents of the note, that she thought Jim had too much good sense to start off for Canada without first finding out from Grandfather the best and safest way to get there.

Robbie insisted that he never would have left them without even saying good-by. And from the moment he laid his eyes on the penciled scrawl which David had found on the bench beside Jim's bed, Grandfather was suspicious of it.

"It looks like Jim's handwriting, all right," Grandfather declared, studying the note by the light from the kitchen window, "but I'm certain the lad could never spell all those words without help, and —"

"It's that sneaking old Snively!" David interrupted wrathfully. "He's copied Jim's writing and left that note to fool us, and he's carried Jim off. He'll sell him somewhere, Grandpa. I know he will, and it's all my fault."

In a voice choking with excitement and unhappiness, David blurted out the story of the talk with Mr. Snively, and then described the noises he had heard early that morning.

"He told Nancy and me he was our friend," the boy finished miserably, "and he's nothing but a liar and a sneaking old slave catcher. He'll sell — he'll sell —" David could not go on. Brushing away the tears which had rushed to his eyes, he swung around on his heel and started to open the kitchen door.

"Hey! Where are you going, lad?" Grandfather asked sharply.

"To get a horse," David answered in a muffled tone. "Mr. Adams at the Tremont House will give me one. I'll chase that old Snively and —"

In three strides Grandfather had crossed the room.

"Don't take leave of your senses, Dave," he said quietly, grasping David by the arm. "Snively has such a head start now that even if we knew which way he went we couldn't overtake him. And suppose we did find him? Then what? Why, he can claim poor Jim is a runaway and that he's just carrying him back to his master, and the law —"

"But Grandpa, we have to do something. Jim's my friend. We have to do *something!*" David cried, his voice rising on the last word. Then turning to his mother, who was watching him with a puzzled frown, he added, half sobbing, "We must help Jim! Oh, Ma, we *must* help him! Isn't there *anything* we can do?"

"Not about poor Jim, I'm afraid," Mrs. Morgan replied, stepping up to David and laying her hand against his forehead. "It's high time we did something about you, though. You're burning up with fever, son."

She sighed. "It's measles, as sure as my name is Susan Morgan. And you might just as well have them right along in the same room with Robbie and Peter. So bring your bedclothes and come on upstairs."

And although David protested again and again that he wasn't sick at all and that he must do something about Jim, she made him go upstairs. Soon she had him tucked warmly into his own bed, which Grandfather had been occupying ever since Mr. Snively's arrival.

Some boys are lucky when they have the measles and are not very sick. That's the way it was with Peter, who was up and playing in the back yard only a week after he had first been put to bed. Robbie, on the other hand, did not recover quite so quickly, probably because of his ducking in Lake Michigan. And David was very ill — first with a high fever and then with an earache which finally became so bad that Grandfather had to go out late one night to get a doctor.

Strangely enough, Nancy never caught the disease, and this was fortunate for everyone. For with the three boys sick, Jim gone, and no one to help with the chores and run errands, the work piled up. Indeed, if Grandfather had not given up his writing and turned nurse and store tender, Mother and Nancy would never have been able to get through those days without closing the shop.

Even after the younger children were up and about, old Mr. Morgan sat hour after hour beside David's bed, putting cool, wet cloths on the boy's hot head, changing the onion poultices on his aching ear, giving him his medicine, and trying to quiet him when he became restless or worried about Jim.

Sometimes he read David chapters from the big family Bible, or from *The Last of the Mohicans*, which David had begun many days earlier. At other times he read him bits from the newspaper about the new Pony Express, which had just begun to carry mail from San Francisco all the way to St. Joseph, Missouri, in only ten days. Or about a young man named Lowe, who was planning to cross the Atlantic Ocean in a big balloon, with a small steamboat attached which would carry him to shore if the whole thing fell into the sea.

And once Grandfather read aloud a letter which he had just received from David's eighteen-year-old cousin, Jed Butler, who had gone with a party of ten men in a covered wagon to Pikes Peak in Colorado, in search of gold. Jed wrote that he had killed two buffalo and lived for several days in an Indian village, but that he had found no gold yet and thought it would be many months before he returned to his home in St. Louis, Missouri.

Of course Grandfather and David and everyone else in the Morgan family talked often about Jim, Mr. Snively, and the whole unhappy subject of slavery. Grandfather blamed himself bitterly because he had not found out more about Mr. Snively's business before letting him live so long in the Morgans' house.

Robbie said that if only he hadn't run off and gone fishing, Jim might still be with them. Nancy wept a few tears privately over the fact that she had helped to give away Jim's secret. And David was more unhappy than any of them over the ill fortune which had befallen his friend and the part he had played in sending Jim back into slavery. For everyone was quite sure now that Snively had carried Jim away.

Three things had happened which left little doubt about this. First, Mother had discovered that the wooden box which Jim had been using for a bank was still on the shelf over his bed and still contained the money the boy had been saving for new clothes. Certainly, she said, if Jim had been going to Canada he would have taken his money with him.

Secondly, when Nancy cleaned the room which Mr. Snively had been occupying, she found Jim's copybook rolled up tightly and wedged between the bureau and the wall. No one knew when or how Snively had taken the copybook from the shed, but everyone knew why, and agreed that the trick he had tried to play was a stupid one.

And thirdly, the day after Jim disappeared, Grandfather had come across a story in a newspaper which told how two men had tried to arrest and carry back to slavery a young colored woman who had been working at the Richmond Hotel. The woman had escaped and had been sent on to Canada by friends. But the newspaper had carried a warning that the slave catchers might still be about, and had given a description of the two men, so that all colored people in Chicago might be wary of them. One of those men was a marshal from Tennessee. From the description of the other, there was no doubt that he was Adelbert Snively.

It was the name "Tennessee" which lingered in David's mind after Grandfather read him this newspaper story, nearly three weeks later, as the boy sat up in bed with two pillows at his back and his breakfast tray on his knees.

"Do you think that's where Snively has taken Jim?" David asked soberly, sopping up the last bit of egg with a small piece of bread.

"Perhaps," Grandfather replied. "But he may have sold him there to someone who'll take him farther south."

"Jim will run away, wherever he is," David declared,

draining the last drops of milk from his pewter mug. "He'll run away and try to get to the North again. Don't you think he will?"

Grandfather sighed as he folded his paper, stuffed it into his pocket, and picked up the tray which had held David's breakfast. "Of course he'll try," he said. "Jim's a brave lad, and he knows now what freedom means. But running away is dangerous business, even with help from the Underground Railroad." And, shaking his head, the old gentleman went slowly out of the room.

Left alone with his thoughts, David sank back against the pillows, linked his hands behind his head, and stared at the ceiling. "The Underground Railroad!" As he said them to himself, there was almost a magic sound in those words. Once David had thought that they stood for a real railroad which ran in some strange way on tracks deep underground. Now, however, he knew that they stood for something far more mysterious and exciting.

Bob Pinkerton, a friend of his who was just his age and lived not far away on Adams Street, had explained it to him one day. The two boys had been exploring a patch of woodland a mile or so north of the Chicago River, and had stumbled on an abandoned shack, well hidden by the underbrush.

"It's like a hideaway on the Underground Railroad my father told me about," Bob had said. Then, seeing that David looked puzzled, he had added, "You know, that's a kind of secret way some people have of helping slaves escape and get north."

"What people?" David had asked.

"Oh, just people! There are hundreds of them all over the country. My father is one of them," Bob had replied proudly, squatting down on the ground at the entrance of the shack. "It works this way: Suppose you are a slave running away from your master, and a man you've never seen before finds you hiding in his haystack. If that man thinks it's all right to own slaves or wants to get a reward, he'll try to catch you and take you back to your master. If he doesn't like slavery, but is too scared to do anything about it, he'll probably pretend he doesn't see you and go away. But if he hates slavery and is very brave, he'll take you home and hide you when slave catchers come looking for you. He'll feed you, too, and give you clothes, and then he'll smuggle you on to another place, farther north, where people feel the same way about slavery that he does. Those people will help you get still farther north, — and — well, that's the Underground Railroad!"

David would have liked to talk longer at this time about the Underground, but Bob, who had tired of the subject, had begun to explore the shack, and nothing more had been said on the matter. Since then this railroad, which wasn't a railroad at all, had seldom been in David's thoughts.

Now, as he lay in bed staring at the ceiling, he began to wish he knew more about it. He wondered if Jim would ever find out about the Underground Railroad. How would Jim know, when he tried to escape, which people would help him and which wouldn't? And what happened to men who helped slaves run away from their owners? Hearing steps outside the door, he turned to ask his grandfather these questions. But it was Nancy, not Mr. Morgan, who entered the room.

"Look," she exclaimed, waving a piece of paper at her brother. "Robbie's just fetched the mail from the post office, and here's a nice letter from Mr. Taylor with the copy of Jim's certificate of freedom." Perching herself on the edge of the bed, she handed her brother the letter. Almost immediately, however, she snatched it back. "I'm sorry! I forgot!" she exclaimed. "Mother says you mustn't read yet. The doctor told her it's bad for your eyes."

David grinned and burrowed deeper into his pillows. "Don't want to read it, anyway," he declared, just to be contrary. Then, in a more serious tone, he added, "It's come too late to help Jim, unless —" He stopped and scratched his nose thoughtfully.

"Unless what?" Nancy asked.

"Unless I can get it to him some way," David went on sitting up in bed and leaning forward eagerly. "Listen, Nance, Jim will send word to us somehow to let us know where he is. I'm sure of that. And when he does I —"

"When he does — and if he does — we'll all do everything we can to bring him safely north," Mother remarked, appearing suddenly on the threshold. "In the meantime, Dave, if you want to get up for a while this afternoon, lie down this minute and pull the covers over you." With a firm hand she tucked the bedclothes around David's shoulders. Then she sent Nancy downstairs to put Jim's certificate in Grandfather's desk and set about tidying the room.

That afternoon David sat up for a while in a chair by the window. And the following day, though his knees were still wobbly and he felt a bit lightheaded, he went downstairs for supper. Nancy had decorated the table with June roses which one of the neighbors had brought in, and Mother had made a special cake with snow-white icing to celebrate the occasion.

"It's like a birthday, except there are no presents," Peter announced, as he moved his chair a little closer to David's.

Robbie fished in his pocket. "There are, too, presents," he said, pulling out a grubby-looking little package and handing it to his eldest brother. "Here, Davy, it's for you."

"What is it?" David asked curiously, beginning to tear off the paper which Robbie had wrapped around and around something hard and flat. Then, before Robbie could answer, he cried out in amazement, "Why, it's money! A whole silver dollar! Where did you get it, Rob?"

"Found it," Robbie replied, his eyes shining with joy over his brother's surprise. "Under the wooden sidewalk over on Clark Street, where they're lifting up those buildings. I was just crawling around looking for a baby rat to tame, and there was this dollar lying in the mud. So I brought it home and shined it up, and it's all for you."

He leaned affectionately against David's shoulder, beaming proudly as David showed the coin to the rest of the family, who had gathered around to exclaim over the gift. "It's a lot of money," he added wistfully. "Fourth of July is coming soon. It would buy a big heap of fireworks."

David nodded. "I know it," he agreed. "But — well, if nobody minds, I'd like to save it for Jim. When he lets us know where he is, we'll need some extra money to help him with, maybe, and —" He looked around at Robbie. "Would that be all right, Robbie?" he asked.

"Yes," Robbie said slowly, trying to keep the disappointment out of his voice and to remember that the dollar was a gift. "Yes, I think that's a good idea."

So the silver coin was put safely away in a little pasteboard box. David made a slit in the cover of the box and wrote "For Jim" on one side. Nancy suggested that everyone drop money through the slit whenever he could, and Mother put the homemade bank on the lowest closet shelf where even little Peter could reach it.

At first, whenever they had pennies, the younger boys added them to the slowly growing fund of money in the box, feeling very virtuous each time they did so. But as weeks went by and no word came from Jim, they began to forget him. So did Nancy. Even David, though he still felt sure that someday he would see Jim again, thought less and less about his friend as

June faded into July and August came, bringing hot days and breathless nights to the city.

The summer months passed swiftly, for there were so many things to do and think about. Despite the fact that David had managed to get a job as an errand boy in McClurg's big bookstore and was helping in the shop at home, he found time nearly every day to go swimming with the boys in the neighborhood. There were picnics now and then in the country or on the white sandy beach south of Chicago, to which all the family went, and band concerts in Dearborn Park, and boat trips on the lake. And then there were the Wide-Awakes!

Night after night in many northern cities that summer and fall, the Wide-Awakes — groups of young men who were determined that Abraham Lincoln would become the next President of the United States — were marching, waving Lincoln banners, and singing Lincoln songs. Dressed in shiny black capes and fine peaked caps trimmed with red, white, and blue, thousands of Chicago Wide-Awakes paraded through the streets of the city to the stirring music of trumpets, fifes, and drums.

"We are coming, we are coming," they sang lustily, as they marched along, swinging gay-colored lanterns and lighting the darkened thoroughfares with blazing torches held high.

> We are coming, we are coming,
> Freedom's battle has begun.

And inscribed upon our banner
Is the name of Abe Lincoln.

And our voice which swells for Lincoln
And for freedom evermore
Shall be hailed by land and seamen
As was never heard before.

We will vote for old Abe Lincoln
We will vote for old Abe Lincoln
We're for honest old Abe Lincoln
And for freedom through the land.

Little chills of excitement ran up and down David's spine whenever he heard the Wide-Awakes singing this song and watched them tramping along the streets, turning night to day with their lanterns and torches. He learned the words and tune of the song and he taught them to Peter and Robbie, who marched around the back yard or up and down State Street with the other small boys in the neighborhood, brandishing sticks for torches, and dressed in capes made from their mothers' outworn petticoats and dresses.

One evening early in October, David even borrowed a Wide-Awake songbook from Bob Pinkerton's older brother and began to copy the words of another song. Except for Robbie and Peter, who were sound asleep in bed, and Inky, who was curled up near the stove purring contentedly, he was alone in the house. For Grandfather was attending a lecture at Metropolitan

Hall, Nancy was at singing school, and Mother had gone to a quilting party at the church.

Dipping his quill pen into Grandfather's old leather ink bottle, which he had set out on the kitchen table, David carefully copied one verse of the song, saying the words to himself as he set them down.

> Oh, hear you not the wild huzzas
> That come from every state?
> For honest Uncle Abraham
> The people's candidate,

He wrote slowly, moving his paper closer to the coal-oil lamp, as a gust of wind blew down the chimney and set the flame flickering.

> He is our choice, our nominee,
> A self-made man and —

"Oh, drat it!" he exclaimed aloud. "Now I've made a blot." He began to blow gently on the smudge of ink to dry it. Then suddenly he raised his head. Someone had rapped softly three times — not on the door, but on the window close beside him.

"Who's there?" David asked in a startled voice. With a thumping heart he picked up the lamp and started toward the window. As he did so the mysterious rapping came again. This time the boy caught sight of a brown hand.

"Jim!" he cried joyfully. With the lamp still in his hand, he went to the door, pulled it open, and peered into the darkness. "Jim!" he exclaimed softly. "Is it you? Come in."

But it was not Jim who slipped past him through the open door, like a shadow out of the night.

chapter *7*

Plans for a Rescue

S TILL HOLDING the lamp in his hand, and with his
heart beating loudly, David stared at the brown-
skinned stranger who stood before him.

"Who are you?" he asked. "What do you want in
here?"

The man did not reply. Glancing quickly around
the room as if to make sure that there was no one else
about, he questioned in a low tone, "Is you David
Morgan?"

David nodded, swallowing hard. Then he stepped
aside as the man brushed past him, stuck his head
through the still open door and said in a half whisper,
"All right, Dora, we's safe."

"Sure enough, Mark?" a voice in the dark asked
timidly.

"Sure enough," the man replied, and led into the room a woman dressed in black, with a heavy black veil hanging from her bonnet.

With a quick movement the woman threw the veil back from her brown face, removed the bonnet, and drew a deep breath. The man called Mark smiled shyly at David.

"Soon as I done hear you call out 'Jim,' I knew we was safe," he said.

"Jim?" David repeated rather stupidly, still so surprised by his unexpected and unknown visitors that he could not pull his wits together.

"Yes, sir," Mark continued. "He done tole us how to git here, and he said your grandpappy would help us maybe to git to Canada, and — " Mark stopped abruptly and slipped an arm around the woman, who had shut her eyes and was swaying slightly back and forth.

"There, Dora," he said gently, reaching for a chair with his free hand, "you set down, honey. The young gentleman won't mind." Turning to David he added apologetically, "My poor wife done had a real hard time since we started north, and she's plumb wore out."

David came suddenly to his senses. These were runaways, and they were Jim's friends. Poor Dora was so tired that she was faint, and probably both of them were starving. Setting the lamp on the table, David stepped quickly to the window and lowered the shade. Although he was bursting with curiosity about Jim, he decided that food must come before questions.

"I'll bet you're both hungry," he remarked. And pulling open the door of the cupboard, he took from the shelves a loaf of fresh bread, a platter on which there were several slices of cold pork left from dinner, and half an apple pie. He put them on the table with some plates, knives, and forks, explaining as he laid these things in place that his grandfather, mother, and sister were all away but would be home soon.

"Here," he said, "sit down and have some supper. I'll go down cellar for some milk." Waiting only long enough to see Mark help his wife to the table, he lighted a candle and started down the cellar stairs. He was back very soon, balancing a plate of butter on top of a pitcher full of milk and carrying a slab of cheese in the same hand that held the candle.

Mark and Dora ate timidly at first, glancing here and there about the room as if they were afraid of being watched. Then, gaining courage as David urged them to eat, they fell to with a will, and the food disappeared as if by magic. Not until the last bite of pork and the last crumb of pie had vanished did David come out with the question which was uppermost in his mind.

"Where's Jim?" he asked, leaning his elbows on the table and looking curiously from Dora to Mark.

"On Mr. Cooper's tobaccy farm in Greenfield. That's in Missouri," Mark answered, wiping his mouth on the back of his hand. "When we run off, he was aimin' to come with us. Fact is, me and Dora wouldn't have tried to git away if it wasn't for Jim. He kep' tellin' us how grand it was to be free, an' plannin' how we three would git north to Canada. And then on the night we snuck off, poor Jim, he stepped into a hole 'fore we even got clear of Mr. Cooper's land, and hurt his leg so bad he couldn't hardly walk."

Mark shook his head sadly, and Dora took up the story.

"He wouldn't even let me tie it up for him with a piece of my pettiskirt," she said softly. "Jes' sat there in the dark, beggin' us to go on an' sayin' he'd git back to his cabin somehow afore daylight."

"An' beggin' us to git to you and your grandpappy," Mark added, "so's we could tell you where he is. Maybe his freedom paper has come, he says, an' —"

Jumping suddenly to his feet, Mark looked hastily around the room, his eyes filled with terror, for the bell over the front door had jangled softly.

"Hide us, quick," he begged, putting an arm around Dora. "Someone is acomin'. Hide us."

"It's only my grandfather," David said reassuringly, as he recognized the step in the hall. "Don't be frightened." And pushing back his chair, David went into the hallway to tell his grandfather of their unexpected guests.

Despite David's assurances and all that they had heard from Jim about the kindness of the Morgan family, both Dora and Mark were still trembling with fear when Grandfather and David entered the kitchen. Mr. Morgan soon put the fugitives at their ease, however, and before long Mark was telling the story of

their escape from Greenfield.

They had traveled only at night, he said, hiding in the woods through the daytime, living on food which they had brought along for the journey and water from the streams they came upon now and then.

" 'Ceptin' for bein' scared, we made out all right till the fourth day," Mark said. "Then Dora, she got the toothache so bad she couldn't hardly speak, an' our food give out, and we couldn't seem to find that Mississippi River. We jes' didn't know where we was or what we was goin' to do."

Mark hesitated and laid his hand on his wife's knee, as if comforting her for the troubles through which she had passed.

"What happened then?" David prompted eagerly.

"What happened then was mos' wonderful," Dora said in her soft voice. "Mos' wonderful. We was hidin' there in the bushes, and all of a sudden the biggest black dog I ever seen come pokin' along and seen us and set up a barkin' you could hear a mile. We knew it weren't no use to run, and reckoned we was caught for sure an' —"

"An' jes' then a man came through the bushes," Mark interrupted. "A colored man, jes' like us. 'You runnin' away?' he asked. 'I'll help you.' An' he took us to his cabin an' fed us, an' give Dora somethin' for her tooth, an' that night he drove us in a wagon to friends of his — white folks. We didn't have any real awful bad trouble any more, 'cause from then on we was travelin' by the Underground Railroad."

"An' now —" Mark drew a deep breath. "An' now," he repeated, looking hopefully from Grandfather to David, "we has reached the last stop afore we gits to Canada an' is truly free."

Grandfather nodded soberly. "That's right," he said. "I'll find out tonight from our friend, Mr. Pinkerton, when the next boat is sailing for Canada with a captain we can trust." He rose from his chair. Wrapping his shawl around his shoulders and putting on his tall hat, he set out shortly for the house of Mr. Allan Pinkerton — a famous detective in Chicago who had run a station on the Underground Railroad for many years and had helped a great number of Negroes escape to freedom.

Dora began to gather up the dishes she and Mark had used. By the time Mrs. Morgan and Nancy came home half an hour later every trace of the meal had disappeared, and Mark was telling David all about Jim and about Mr. Cooper's tobacco farm in Greenfield.

Hardly had Mother and Nancy entered the house and been told who Mark and Dora were, when Grandfather returned. He reported that by great good fortune a boat commanded by a friendly captain was sailing early the following morning for a Canadian port.

"I have a hack waiting outside," he said. "You must get aboard as soon as possible. Mr. Pinkerton told me that only this afternoon the boat was searched by a sheriff looking for runaways. But the captain will stow you away in the hold until you reach Canada. He's a fine man, and you can trust him absolutely."

"They can't go without food," Mother said quickly. And she bustled around the kitchen, putting up a lunch, while David filled a small jug with water from the pump and Nancy scurried about looking for a pair of boots which would fit Dora, whose shoes were quite worn out.

Poor Dora had begun to tremble again at the thought of leaving this friendly household and embarking for a strange land. But she tried to smile as she said her thank-you's and good-by's, clinging all the time to her husband's arm.

"You'll help Jim somehow, sure enough?" Mark asked just before he turned to follow Grandfather, who was waiting impatiently at the door.

"We'll do all we can," Mother promised. Nancy nodded her head and David said, "We'll get him north someway, Mark, now we know where to find him."

Mark smiled gratefully. A moment later the fugitives were gone.

The lamps burned late in the Morgan house that night as David repeated all that Mark had told him about Jim, and the Morgans sat in Grandfather's room discussing how they could best help their young friend. Mother suggested that Jim's freedom paper be mailed to him at once. But Grandfather pointed out that slaves seldom, if ever, received mail directly, and that the paper probably would never reach him.

"Without a doubt, Mr. Cooper receives all the mail sent to people on his plantation," Grandfather said. "A letter from the North addressed to Jim would just get the lad in trouble, especially since two of Mr. Cooper's slaves have just escaped."

"Would the certificate be of any use to Jim in Missouri, even if he had it?" Mother asked doubtfully.

Grandfather tugged at his beard. "No," he said slowly. "I think not. According to the law, Jim is now the property of Mr. Cooper, who probably paid a good price for him. A certificate signed by Mr. Taylor of Kentucky won't mean anything.

"But once the lad gets into Illinois, the certificate may help him, if slave hunters or sheriffs catch up with him. At any rate, the freedom paper is his, and so is the money he saved when he was working on the Wigwam. We must get them both to him as soon as we can."

"How?" asked Nancy.

"I'll take them to him, of course," David said eagerly. "I can get there some way and —"

Grandfather interrupted. "Look here," he said, pointing to a spot on the big wall map which hung behind his desk, "here's Greenfield. It's not much more than fifty miles as the crow flies, northwest of St. Louis. If Jed Butler were only home, instead of gallivanting around in the West hunting for gold, we could send him the certificate and money, and trust him to get them to Jim, but —"

"But he isn't," David put in. He looked beseechingly from his mother to his grandfather and back again. "Let me take them," he begged. "Oh, please let me."

Mother shook her head. "I want Jim to be free just

as much as you do, Davy, but I'll not have you setting out on any such wild-goose chase as this one," she said decidedly. "You're not old enough yet to go traipsing around the country."

"He won't be traipsing around the country, Susan!" Grandfather exclaimed, rather testily. "I see no reason at all why he shouldn't go, if we can scrape together enough money to send him. After all, he's nearly thirteen and, as I see it, all he has to do is ride on the steam cars as far as Alton, take a ferry to St. Louis, and go to the Butlers'. They're Abolitionists — though not many people in St. Louis know it — and they'll break their necks to help the boy get on to Greenfield when they know why he wants to go there. Carl Butler will probably take him all the way to Cooper's farm, himself."

"But suppose —" Mother began.

David spoke up before she had time to complete her sentence. "Let me go, Ma," he pleaded. "I'll do just what Uncle Carl tells me to. I'll be careful and — oh, please let me go."

He spoke so earnestly that Nancy added her pleading to his. And with Grandfather insisting that boys no older than David had often taken far longer, more difficult trips, and that the family owed it to Jim to get help to him as quickly as possible, Mother was forced at last to give in.

When David crawled between the sheets that night, after a long discussion of ways and means, he was so excited he could not go to sleep. Again and again he went over the plans which Mother and Grandfather had made for his journey.

He was to leave Chicago just as soon as Grandfather could get together enough money for the trip. The train which left the city at nine in the morning would reach Springfield at nine minutes after five that evening, providing that all went well.

Although that same train went right on to Alton, connecting with the ferry there for St. Louis, David was to stop off in Springfield and spend the night there with his Aunt Hattie. This part of the arrangement seemed very foolish to the boy, who was anxious to get to Jim as soon as he could. But Mother insisted that she did not want David to arrive in a strange city the size of St. Louis after dark, and Grandfather seemed to think the plan a good one.

"I'll write a letter to your Aunt Hattie and another to the Butlers and mail them at once, telling them to expect you whenever you can get there, but not why you are coming," Grandfather had said. "Your Aunt Hattie is a great talker, and it will be better if she does not know the reason you are making this journey. As for the Butlers, you can tell them anything and trust them absolutely. From the time you reach their home in St. Louis, whatever you do will be up to them and to you."

"Whatever you do! Whatever you do!" The words said themselves over and over again in David's mind. They were all mixed up somehow with a dark face belonging to a man named Mark, and a soft voice saying,

"Mos' wonderful!"

Hardly conscious of what he was doing, David reached for the extra blanket at the foot of his bed and pulled it up under his chin. The next thing he knew, it was morning.

chapter 8

Off to a Bad Start

DAVID sat bolt upright on the hard, red, plush-covered seat, his flowered carpetbag at his feet, his box of lunch beside him, and his ticket for Springfield in his pocket.

Just outside the car window, close to his right elbow, the entire Morgan family stood waiting on the dingy platform of the Randolph Street depot to call a final good-by. Mother was smiling at David and dabbing at her eyes with her handkerchief. Nancy was trying to dissuade Peter from crawling under the steam cars to examine the brakes. And Grandfather, who had a firm grasp on Robbie's collar, was saying something through the closed window that David could neither hear nor understand.

Inside the car people were bustling about finding seats, stowing away bags and baskets, and settling themselves for the journey. A baby had begun to cry, and a little boy in a flat felt hat was pushing his way in and out among the people in the aisle, calling his mother.

A red-faced conductor in a blue uniform trimmed with gold braid stood on the platform close to the car steps, peering at his watch.

"All aboard!" he yelled. "All aboard for Joliet, Bloomington, Springfield, Carlinville, and Alton. 'Board!"

In answer to his cry, a fat woman, who was trying to hold a large feathered bonnet on her head with one hand and carry a heavy basket with the other, began to run toward the train, her hoopskirt swaying back and forth and her yellow curls bobbing up and down with every step. A tall, red-bearded man swung a chunky little girl off her feet, kissed her hastily, and set her down, as the conductor shouted once again, "'Board! All aboard!" and the bell on the engine clanged noisily.

Suddenly, with no warning at all, the train jerked forward violently, jerked again, stopped, jerked and stopped, and then with a final lurch and shiver began to move slowly ahead.

"We're off," David thought, with a strange fluttery feeling in the pit of his stomach.

Pressing his nose close to the glass, he waved his hand at the little group outside the car window, mak-

ing his lips frame the words "Good-by! Good-by!"
Mother and Nancy waved their handkerchiefs excitedly. And Grandfather, with a small boy on either
side, limped along beside the car until the engine had
gained so much speed that he could no longer keep
pace with it.

With the bell still ringing, the steam whistle tooting
a warning, and the wheels making a hollow, rumbling
sound, the train began its journey over the long trestle
just inside the breakwater. Glancing through one of
the windows across the narrow aisle, David glimpsed
the water of Lake Michigan, whipped into whitecaps
by a stiff October breeze, and saw spray rise high into
the air from the breakers which pounded against the
rocks.

On his own side of the car lay the lagoon, the sandy
beach, and beyond the beach, the streets of Chicago.
Peering out eagerly for a last glimpse of the city, David
named the streets to himself, as they slid past the window. Washington Street with all its church spires
gleaming in the sun; Madison Street where the wealthy
people lived; Monroe Street next, with homes which
were not quite so fine; Adams Street, where cows were
pastured in vacant lots and chickens scratched in the
dust; Jackson Street, lined with tiny homes and ramshackle shanties; Van Buren Street, Congress Street,
Harrison — they were in real country now, with farms
and fields and patches of woodland on either side of
the track.

"Looks right pretty, even though the leaves are

dropping, don't it?" said a voice close to David's ear. Looking around sharply, David saw that a little old woman in a poke bonnet, with a gray shawl wrapped around her shoulders and worn black gloves on her folded hands, was sitting on the narrow seat beside him. She nodded her head in a friendly fashion and seemed eager to go on talking. But David only smiled politely and turned again to the window. He had so many things to think about that he was not yet ready to open a conversation with anyone.

With an uneasy feeling that he had forgotten something, he checked over the things he was supposed to have with him. He knew that Jim's money and certificate of freedom were in the inside of his coat, sewn in by Nancy so that they could not be lost.

His own money, in a flat leather purse with strong brass clasps, was in the right-hand pocket of his pantaloons. There was a neatly folded piece of paper in that purse also, with the Butlers' address in St. Louis and a funny-looking map Mother had drawn, showing him how to get from the depot in Springfield to Aunt Hattie's house.

Tucked between the cover of his box of lunch and the string which held it together was a letter which Grandfather had written for him to read on the train. And when he lifted his carpetbag to his lap and looked inside, he found a small gray book, lying right where he knew it should be. It was the dictionary which belonged to Mr. Abraham Lincoln.

"What with the excitement over Jim's bad luck, and

the measles, and all the other things that have happened recently, I never did get this mailed," Grandfather had explained, showing the book to David, just as the boy was closing his bag that morning. "You'll have plenty of time this evening in Springfield to leave it at the Lincolns' house, and I'll be glad to know it's in the hands of its rightful owner at last." Then he had stuck the book in the bag on top of David's yellow nightshirt.

David shifted the book a little to one side, shut the bag, and started to set it down at his feet again. Suddenly, with whistle screeching and the glass lamp, which hung from the center of the roof, swaying back and forth, the train lurched around a curve. The flowered carpetbag spilled to the floor, and David almost fell over into the lap of the passenger beside him.

"Land's sakes! We're going real fast!" the little old lady commented, smiling as David righted himself and apologized.

"Near twenty-five miles an hour," a bespectacled gentleman sitting across the aisle remarked sharply. "It's scandalous — that's what it is! No regard for life or limb and —"

Grabbing wildly at the arm of his seat — for the train had swerved again — the gentleman sank back with a grim look on his face.

The little old lady fished in her bag, took out a pepperment, popped it into her mouth, and folded her hands again demurely. All at once David realized that he was hungry. He had been so excited at breakfast time over the thought of his trip that he had eaten hardly anything at all.

"I'll just have a couple of doughnuts now and save the rest of my lunch till noon time," he thought. "Might as well read Grandpa's letter now, too, I reckon."

So he unfastened the string on his box, took out two doughnuts, and ate them slowly as trees and hills, farms and little villages, slid past the window. Then, wiping his hands carefully on his handkerchief, he opened his grandfather's letter.

"Jingoes, it's a long one!" he exclaimed, half-aloud.

And settling back in his seat, he unfolded several sheets of paper covered with his grandfather's spidery handwriting, crossed one knee over the other, and began to read.

The letter was dated at the top October 21, 1860, just as if Grandfather had intended to send it through the mail.

"My dear David," it began,

Tomorrow you will be setting out on your journey to Greenfield. There are several things which I had hoped to talk over with you before you left. But there semed no opportunity for us to talk alone, and because I see no sense in worrying your mother about the matters I have in mind, I shall write about them.

If you have the gumption I think you have, I feel sure that you are planning not only to get Jim's paper and money to him, but to help him escape. And that may be dangerous business, even with your Uncle Carl's help. You will need to keep your wits about you at all times and your eyes open.

Guard your tongue, too. Don't talk big or boast to anyone that you are from the North, or that Northerners are better than Southerners because they don't keep slaves. Remember that many Northerners kept slaves, too, not so very many years ago. Remember also that thousands of Southerners have never owned slaves, even when they could afford to do so.

There is, right now, a great deal of hard feeling between the North and the South. This is partly because so many slaves have escaped to the North and have never been returned to their masters. It is also partly because many slaveowners are eager to move into the new lands which are being opened in the West, and to set up more slave states. And people in the North who hate slavery are trying to prevent them from doing so.

Already there has been bitter fighting about this. Now, men in South Carolina are threatening to withdraw from the Union and to set up their own government if anyone who is against the spreading of slavery is elected President. True Americans will never allow the United States to be broken up in this way for any reason. So I fear we may be headed toward a civil war. Therefore, waste no time on your journey. We shall want you safe at home in Chicago if any real trouble breaks out.

Now, about the matter of money. You —

"Ticket, please!" A man's voice and a tap on the shoulder interrupted David's reading. "May I have your ticket, young man, or money for your passage?"

"Yes, sir," David said. Fumbling in his pocket, he fished out the ticket Grandfather had bought for him and handed it to the conductor.

"Hmm! Another for Springfield!" the conductor exclaimed. "Seems everybody's bound for there since Mr. Lincoln has become so important. Are you aimin' to see Mr. Lincoln, too, bub?" He laughed, as if he considered this a great joke, and raised his eyebrows in mock surprise when David answered quietly, "Yes sir, I aim to see Mr. Lincoln."

As the conductor started down the aisle, David felt his carpetbag just to be sure that the dictionary was still there, and his heart beat faster at the thought of meeting the man who might someday be President of the United States.

He was trying to think out what he would say when he first met Mr. Lincoln, when suddenly, with a great screeching of brakes, the train came to an abrupt stop. The ticket taker fell sprawling against the seat, a pretty girl in a blue ruffled hoopskirt sat down unexpectedly on the floor, and the other passengers were shaken up unmercifully.

"Now what?" mumbled the conductor, pulling down his jacket and helping the girl to her feet. "What in all tarnation's happened now?" Still muttering, he went toward the front of the car to investigate.

He was back before very long.

" 'Tain't anything much," he announced to the passengers, who were looking nervously out of the windows on both sides of the car. "Just hit a cow — that's all. We'll be on our way in a minute."

At that very instant, the train jerked forward so suddenly that once more the poor man was hurled against a seat. Swearing under his breath, he straightened his cap, which had fallen over his eyes, and went on down the aisle. As the engine gained speed and chugged on through the countryside, David settled back in his seat and went on with his letter.

"Now, about the matter of money," Grandfather had written,

> . . . you have barely enough for your journey, even if you manage well. I wish I had been able to give you more, but this is the best I can do. Yet I would not have you give up helping Jim just because we are short of funds. I am beginning to have great faith in your ability to take care of yourself. And there are always odd jobs everywhere by which an up-and-coming lad like you can earn a few extra dollars, if necessary. So I shall try not to worry on that score.
>
> The lamp is growing dim and I must stop. Write to us without fail when you reach St. Louis. God bless you and bring you and Jim both back to us safely.
>
> Your loving Grandfather.

David folded the letter thoughtfully, stuck it in his pocket, and gazed out of the window at the little village through which the train was passing. He wasn't worried about money at all. With the fifteen dollars Grandfather had given him, and the two dollars and ten cents which had been saved in the box marked "for Jim," and the three dollars and forty cents he had been able to save from his own wages, it seemed to him that he had a small fortune.

Putting his grandfather's letter out of his mind, he let his thoughts race ahead to the adventures which lay before him. Going to Springfield was to be an adventure in itself, he decided, and he was glad now that Mother had insisted that he stop there. At almost every depot, people got on the train who were going there to see Mr. Lincoln.

There were farmers with their butternut jeans tucked into their high leather boots. And well-dressed gentlemen who talked in low tones about politics as they complained of the cinders which were soiling their white linen, or wondered whether they could get places to stay in crowded Springfield. And ladies who hoped to get a glimpse of Mrs. Lincoln and her home and children. The excitement grew as the train filled to overflowing, and arguments over the coming election broke out.

David didn't know what many of the arguments were about, but he pricked up his ears and thought about Jim every time he heard slavery mentioned. And as he gazed at the passing scenery through the grimy car window, he dreamed up a dozen ways in which he and Uncle Carl would get Jim's certificate to him, and rescue him from Mr. Cooper's tobacco farm.

Hour after hour the steam cars rattled over the iron rails, stopping now and then with much jerking and puffing and squealing of brakes at the depot in some good-sized village or town. The car was hot and stuffy.

Yet when one daring passenger opened a window, such a cloud of dirt and cinders blew in that he closed it quickly. By midafternoon it seemed to David that five o'clock would never come. And when at dusk the conductor lit the hanging kerosene lamp and told one of the passengers nearby that the train would be an hour late getting into Springfield, the boy's heart sank.

Smothering a yawn, David slumped down in his seat, wondering sleepily if anyone were missing him at home, and what Mother would cook for supper, and if Robbie or Peter woud remember to feed Inky. Then he began to think about St. Louis, and wondered how he was going to get from there to Greenfield. But it became harder and harder to keep his thoughts in any sort of order, and the next thing he knew someone was shaking him by the shoulder. Blinking his eyes, David looked up into the red face of the conductor.

"You wasn't figurin' on gettin' off in Springfield, was you, bub?" the conductor was asking him.

David nodded, fumbled sleepily for his carpetbag and stood up. The conductor put a hand on his shoulder.

"Sit down again, lad," he said. "You've no need to hurry. We passed that stop near two hours ago."

"Passed it!" David echoed stupidly, still half-asleep.

"That's right," the conductor agreed. "I plumb forgot you were gettin' off there, with the train so crowded and all, and I reckon you were sleepin' so sound you didn't hear me yell it out. Since we left there I've been havin' a game of cards in the next car, and well, I —"

He shrugged his shoulders, sat down in the empty seat beside David, and rubbed his nose.

"Looks as if you were in kind of a tight spot, young feller," he went on. "What do you figure you'd better do about it?"

"I don't know," David replied slowly, looking around the dimly lighted car, which now held no more than a dozen people. "Where are we now?"

"Next stop's Alton," the conductor answered. "Know anybody there?"

David shook his head. "I have an aunt and uncle in St. Louis, though," he said.

"First rate!" exclaimed the conductor, getting to his feet. "You'll be all right then. Half these folks are goin' to St. Louis. So when you get to Alton, just follow them to the ferry depot and get aboard the same boat they do."

"Yes, sir," David said, rather forlornly.

The conductor put out his hand. "Reckon I'll have to have some more passage money, bub," he announced. "Three dollars and forty cents — that's the fare from Springfield to St. Louis these days."

"Yes, sir," David said again. Pulling his purse from his pocket, he counted out the necessary money, and handed it to the conductor in exchange for the ticket which he would need on the ferry.

Pocketing the cash and giving David his ticket, the conductor stood up. "Well, I reckon I can get back to my card game now," he said. "Good luck, bub!" And he went off down the aisle, leaving David uneasy, disappointed, and thoroughly disgusted with himself.

Now he'd probably never see Springfield, nor talk
with Mr. Lincoln. Aunt Hattie would wonder, as the
days passed, what had happened to him, and write
to Mother to find out. Mother would be more sure
than ever before that her son was not yet old enough
to take care of himself in the great world. And when
Grandfather learned what had happened, he would be
provoked because David had bungled the first step of
his journey so badly.

All in all, the boy had never felt more lonely or
downhearted. And he was not one bit happier when
he stepped from the paddle-wheel ferryboat to the
wharf in St. Louis sometime later.

There was no moon, and it was so dark that he had
seen little of the Mississippi River about which he had
heard so much. Only a handful of people had made
the trip, and most of them had slept from the time
they embarked until the bell rang to announce that
the landing place had been reached. The only bright
spot on the trip was that one of the passengers — a
man who lived in St. Louis — had been able to tell
him just how to get to the Butlers' house. And David
set out at once along a dimly lighted street to follow
his directions.

"Walk straight ahead two blocks, turn to your left,
and go on until you come to the big church on Walnut
Street," the man had said. "Mr. Butler's house sets
close to the pavement just beyond it. 'Tain't very big,
and it's red brick. You can't miss it."

Repeating these directions to himself, David hurried along the streets, which were now almost deserted because of the late hour. Turning to his left at last, he found the church and the red brick house. Although a light gleamed from behind the curtained window of the house next door, the Butlers' home was dark.

"Everybody's gone to bed," David thought ruefully. "I'll have to wake them up." Lifting the knocker on the front door rather hesitantly, he let it fall with a clatter. When no one came, he knocked again, louder this time, and then again. Next he pounded with his fist on the door. Still there was no answer to his summons.

"Maybe they all sleep at the back and can't hear me," the boy thought. Picking up his carpetbag, he started around the house. But at that very instant a window of the house next door was opened and a shadowy figure leaned over the sill.

"Are you lookin' for Mr. Butler?" a woman's voice called softly.

"Yes, ma'am," David replied, snatching off his cap.

"Well, there isn't anybody home there," the woman said. "Mrs. Butler got word two days ago that her mother was sick, and they've all gone over to Tennessee to look after her. They won't be back for a long time, so you might as well go away and stop making all that rumpus."

Moving back into the house before David had a chance to speak, the woman shut the window with a bang.

Poor David! If she had doused him with a bucketful of cold water he could not have been more startled or dismayed. For a moment he stood, bag in hand, looking uncertainly up and down the empty street. Then, once more, he started toward the rear of the Butlers' house, hoping that he might find a window unlatched perhaps, or some way to get into the house through the cellar.

chapter 9

A Strange
Traveling Companion

T HE PROPRIETOR of Lacey's Eating House scratched his head thoughtfully and blinked at David with owllike eyes.

"Never did see a young feller stow away so much breakfast so fast before," he drawled, looking at the empty plates which were ranged before the boy. "Let's see. That's two orders of ham and eggs and fried potatoes, an' one order of fried chicken an' biscuits with gravy, an' a cup of tea, an' two slabs of pie. Is that right?"

David nodded, and since Lacey's Eating House provided no napkins, wiped his mouth on the back of his hand. "How much is it?" he asked.

"Reckon we can settle for fifty cents," the proprietor

113

said, mopping up some tea from the bare table with the corner of his greasy apron. "If by any chance you ain't got the money — an' I sure hope you ain't — you kin work it out washin' dishes. There's a pile in the kitchen a mile high. My kitchen girl ran off day before yesterday, an' I been without help ever since."

"Oh, I have the money!" David said hastily, taking a silver dollar from his purse and wishing at the same time that he had not spent quite so much of his meager store of cash on one meal.

With an air of disappointment, the proprietor examined the coin. "When I meet a lad as has slept in his clothes an' ain't washed his face in a week, an' has splinters in his hair, then I figger he's run away from home and maybe needs a job," he drawled. "Well — " He shrugged his shoulders. "No harm in askin', anyway. You wait a bit, an' I'll fetch your change." He pocketed the coin and shuffled off toward the kitchen.

Feeling rather uncomfortable, David quickly ran his fingers through his hair in an effort to comb out the bits of wood he hadn't known were there. Then he pulled his jacket straight and tried to brush off his pantaloons.

He had spent a forlorn and uncomfortable night in the woodshed behind the Butlers' house, and when he had awakened he had been so hungry he had thought of little but food. Now, however, he turned his head this way and that, trying to catch a glimpse of his reflection in the fly-stained window beside him, so that he might remove some of the dirt the proprietor had noticed. With a grimy handkerchief he rubbed away the worst of the smudges. Then he glanced around hastily, hoping that no one had been watching him.

There were few people in the restaurant, and no one was looking in his direction but a smooth-faced little man with white hair, who sat at the next table, with an empty coffee cup before him. Trying to hide a smile, he looked at David with twinkling blue eyes and nodded approvingly.

"That's better, lad," he said soberly. "Much better. It does beat all how dirty one gets traveling, doesn't it? Have you come very far?"

"From Chicago," David replied. "That's where I live. But I'm not running away from home the way that man thought I was. Honest, I'm not."

"Didn't think you were," the old man declared, leaving his table and coming to sit opposite David. "You don't act like a runaway. Where are you bound?"

"Greenfield," David said, liking the stranger's kindly face at once. "What's the best way to get there, mister?"

The old gentleman pursed his lips. "Well," he said slowly, "that depends. There are two or three good ways to get to Greenfield." He studied David thoughtfully for a moment as if he were trying to make up his mind about something. Then he asked, "Do you have any friends here in St. Louis?"

"Not right now, sir," David replied, wondering what this had to do with getting to Greenfield. "My aunt and uncle live here, but they've gone away. I found their house all locked up when I came last night. That's why I had to sleep in their woodshed."

The old man smiled. "Lots worse places to sleep then a woodshed," he remarked. "What's your uncle's name?"

"Carl Butler," David replied.

The old man raised his eyebrows. "Heard a man by that name talk at a Wide-Awake rally here not long ago," he said. "Your uncle's a great Lincoln man, isn't he?"

David grinned. "Yes sir," he declared proudly. "Everyone in my family is for Mr. Lincoln." Then, in a perplexed tone he added, "I didn't know there were any Wide-Awakes in Missouri, though. It's a slave state, isn't it, sir?"

"That's right," agreed the old gentleman. "But there are lots of people here in St. Louis who would like to put an end to slavery just the same, and to see Abe Lincoln in the White House." He rubbed his chin and stared thoughtfully into space.

"We're for honest old Abe Lincoln — and for freedom through the land," he said after a moment. "There are men who sing that song here just the way they do farther north."

"I know that song — every word of it," David remarked. Then, with his mind on Jim, he asked again the question which was uppermost in his mind. "Can you please tell me the best way to get to Greenfield?"

"You can go from here to a place called Brinton's

Landing on a Missouri River steamboat, if you have plenty of money and time to spare, and then you can go north by stagecoach," the old man said slowly, flicking a bread crumb from his neat black cravat. "But if you don't have much money and want to get there in a hurry . . ." He hesitated and leaned close to David.

"Tell me, are you the kind of a boy who can keep his mouth shut when he runs into something he doesn't quite understand?" he asked in a low tone.

David looked puzzled. "I don't know," he said. "I reckon I am if — well, if I know that what I don't understand is all right." He squirmed uncomfortably in his chair. "I mean if it isn't something bad, like killing or stealing."

"That's what I mean, too," the old man said. Then, looking steadily at David, he asked, "Do I seem to you like a man you could trust?"

For an instant the boy returned look for look. "Yes," he said at last. "I reckon so." Then quickly and more emphatically he added, "Yes, you look like a man *anybody* could trust."

"Good!" exclaimed the old man. He sat back in his chair. "Now that I know a little bit about you, I'll tell you the best way for you to get to Greenfield. It's to ride along with me!"

"With you!" David exclaimed, hardly daring to believe his ears. "Are you really going to Greenfield?"

"Going there and beyond," the old man said. "I make the trip every now and then, and I'd be glad of your company. But these are uneasy times in this part of the country. It's only fair to warn you that I may run into a bit of trouble on the road. In that case, you can take to your heels and get on the rest of the way by yourself." He pushed back his chair, and picked up his tall hat.

"I'm leaving at noon," he continued, laying a hand on David's shoulder. "Think it over, boy, and if you want to come along, meet me in front of Hasler's Hardware Store on Market Street, near Broadway, at twelve o'clock. I'll be looking for you."

Without giving David a chance to speak, he turned and left the restaurant, just as the proprietor came dawdling back with David's change. David stuck the coins in his pocket and snatched up his cap and bag. Then he hurried outside and looked eagerly up and down the street for the old gentleman. He wanted to overtake him, if possible, and to ask him some more questions about the trip to Greenville. But he could not see him among the men and women who were walking along the street.

"He's a queer old man, with all his questions and his talk about trouble on the road," David said to himself, as he stood on the pavement in front of the restaurant. "But there's something about him I like, and — well, if that's the quickest way to get Jim's freedom paper to him, that's the way I'm going."

Repeating to himself the words, "Hasler's Hardward Store, Market Street, near Broadway, twelve o'clock," he walked slowly down the street, wondering what Mother and Grandfather would think of his decision, and how he would find Jim when he got to Greenfield.

It was a beautiful day. Before long David was whistling softly, as he sauntered along the red-brick pavement in the direction of the river, stopping now and then to peer into shop windows, or to watch the people.

St. Louis, with its splendid brick houses and its fine hotels, was older and more settled than Chicago. David missed the hustle and bustle of his home town. Men and women walked more slowly here, talked more softly, and seemed to have plenty of time to stand about chatting with friends. Even the carriage horses and the mules which pulled the wagons and carts moved as though they had all day to get where they were going.

It was all very peaceful and quiet, and a little disappointing to David, who had expected something more exciting on his first visit to a strange city. He was glad when he reached the river, for there he found noise and confusion enough to satisfy any boy.

Boats of many kinds were moving up and down the yellow Mississippi. The long stone levee was lined with passenger steamers, coal barges, little steam ferries, and big freight boats, moored closely side by side. Negroes were loading some, unloading others, and filling waiting wagons and drays with boxes, bales, and casks.

Passengers who had just arrived on incoming steamers stood about with their luggage piled around them, waiting for hacks or stagecoaches. Other passengers, laden with trunks, carpetbags, bundles, and rolls of bedding, were struggling up the landing stages of outgoing steamers.

Men were shouting orders; bells were clanging; whistles were blowing; people were calling to one another. And over all the noise, a balky mule was braying shrilly while a boy who looked a little like Jim tugged at the animal's bridle and swore at him roundly.

For some time David wandered happily up and down the crowded levee, stopping at last before a Missouri River steamer, to watch while a huge covered wagon was loaded on the lower deck of the boat. No sooner had the wagon been safely stowed aboard than a dozen shabbily dressed Negroes, handcuffed together, two by two, and guarded by a heavyset man with a pistol at his belt, were herded up the gangplank.

"Poor fellers," muttered a shaggy-bearded man who stood near David.

"Where are they going?" David asked, looking after the slaves with eyes which had suddenly grown very solemn. "What have they done?"

"I reckon they ain't done nothin', sonny, except to be born in the wrong place at the wrong time," the man answered. "Chances are they've just been bought by some hemp grower in the western part of the state."

"Oh!" David exclaimed softly. A sudden feeling of dismay swept over him. For the first time he began to wonder what he would do if he learned, in reaching

Greenfield, that Jim had been sold farther south or west.

He had been disappointed, of course, when he had found that the Butlers were not in St. Louis. He had even felt a little sorry for himself when he had been forced to spend a night on their woodshed floor. But he had never fully realized until this very minute that, without his Uncle Carl's help, it would be entirely up to him to find Jim, wherever he was, and to get him safely to Illinois.

With this sobering thought in mind, he turned away from the big paddle-wheel steamer, walked along the levee until he found a place where no boat was moored, and sat down with his feet hanging over the water. Fishing in his pocket, he pulled out Grandfather's letter and read it through twice. Then he opened his carpetbag and found the pencil, paper, and envelopes which Mother had packed for him. Laying his paper on the dictionary which belonged to Mr. Lincoln, he began a letter:

Dear Grandpa and Ma and everybody,
    I was asleep when the train got to Springfeald, so I didn't get off, but I will take the book to Mr. Lincoln on my way home if I can. Please write and tell Aunt Hattie why I didn't get there. Uncle Carl and Aunt Sally aren't here. They went to Tenesee because Aunt Sally's mother is sick. But I have found a friend and he is going to take me to Greenfeald. So don't worry about me. Jim and I will be home soon.

                                        David.

Sticking his letter into one of the envelopes, he addressed it carefully, closed his carpetbag, and scrambled to his feet. Half an hour later, having found the post office in the Customs House on the corner of Third and Olive streets, he was on his way to Hasler's Hardware Store.

He knew by the Customs House clock that it was nearly noon, and he hastened his steps as he turned up Market Street. There was no need to ask the way to Hasler's, once he had crossed Broadway, for he caught sight almost at once of a large sign, reading "Hasler's Hardware Emporium," handing out over the pavement some distance ahead.

A big gray horse with a net over him to keep off the flies, and a peddler's wagon filled with tinware, boxes of drygoods, baskets of dishes, brooms, and mops, stood near the entrance of the store. Except for the peddler himself, who seemed to be sound asleep on the driver's seat, his face well hidden by his broad-brimmed hat, there was no one about.

David set his bag down, stuck his hands in his pantaloon pockets, and leaned against a lamppost, keeping a sharp watch up and down the street for the little old man he had met in the restaurant. A clock nearby boomed twelve long strokes. The peddler straightened up slowly and looked around.

"Ah, there you are," he cried, waving a hand at David. "I felt sure you'd come. Hop up, lad. Hop up and let's get started."

David's mouth dropped open, and he blinked his

eyes in surprise. This man didn't look like the man he had met early that morning. He was more shabbily dressed. His white hair hung untidily about his face. And somehow, in only a few hours, he had grown a dirty-looking long gray beard. Only the blue eyes and the voice were the same.

"Hop up!" the man commanded again, rather impatiently. Then, leaning over, he said in a low tone, "Don't be scared off by a false beard, lad. I need it in my business. Come along, if you're coming."

Completely mystified and very curious, David hesitated. Once more the old man leaned forward.

"Remember," he said, looking steadily at David, "you said this morning that I looked like a man you could trust. I'm still the same man I was then."

"Yes sir," David said doubtfully, still hanging back. Then suddenly before his eyes flashed a picture of the Negro slaves he had seen boarding the boat. Without a word, he tossed his bag into the wagon and climbed up over the wheel.

The old man chuckled. Then he picked up the reins and made a clucking noise with his tongue. Tin pans rattled as the wagon started off.

chapter *10*

Simon Perkins' Secret

Names First," the peddler remarked as the wagon clattered west along Market Street. "If we're going to travel together till we get to Greenfield tomorrow, we'll have to know each other's names. Mine's Simon Perkins. What's yours?"

"David Morgan," David replied, looking out of the corner of one eye at Mr. Perkins' beard, and wondering if perhaps the old man might be slightly crazy.

The peddler put a strong hand on the boy's knee. "You may think I'm a bit queer in the head, lad," he said, as if he were reading David's thoughts. "But I'm not. I'm in a strange business. It's a dangerous business, too, and the less you know about it, the better. I'll tell you this much about it, though — it's a good business."

"But why — ?" David began.

Mr. Perkins shook his head. "I can't tell you why anything," he said. "You'll just have to show as much trust in me as I'm showing in you, in taking you along. When I asked you this morning to ride with me, I didn't intend to travel just this way, but —"

He pulled his horse up suddenly as three little boys, in pursuit of a ball, dashed across the street right under the animal's nose.

"But after I left you I received a message which made me change my plans," he continued, as the horse started up again. "I'm going through to Greenfield just the same, though. Do you still want to come along, even if things may happen on the way that you don't understand?"

David nodded his head slowly. "Yes sir," he said. "I'd like to."

"Good!" exclaimed Mr. Perkins. With a reassuring smile at David, he urged his horse to a trot. "Lots of get-up-and-go in old Nell when it's needed," he remarked, as they rattled around a corner. "Hope we won't need it on this trip, though. What do you think of St. Louis?"

"It's a nice city," David replied, shifting his carpetbag so that he would have more room for his feet. "But I like Chicago better."

Mr. Perkins smiled. "Most of us feel that way about our home places," he said in his slow drawl. "Now, I was born down south in Mississippi, in a little village near Vicksburg, and there's no spot in all the world that will ever look as beautiful to me as that one. Going to be in Greenfield long?"

"No sir," David answered. "My grandfather wants me to come home as soon as I can. I'm only going there to — " He checked himself abruptly, remembering just in time that he might find himself in a great deal of trouble if he discussed his errand with a stranger, especially a stranger who had been born in the South.

Mr. Perkins chuckled. "Don't tell me, if you don't want to," he said. "That's your secret, and I have mine." And, changing the subject, he began to talk about the great fair which had been held in St. Louis the previous week.

Since it was the noon hour and most of the people in St. Louis were at dinner, there was little traffic in the streets. The gray horse clip-clopped along at a good pace. Within a short time David and Mr. Perkins had left the city behind them and were rattling along a winding country road.

Wide meadows, patches of woodland, and prosperous-looking farms lay on either side of them. Children played together under trees which had turned to crimson and gold. Cats slept peacefully on sunny doorsteps. And here and there around the houses and in the fields, David saw Negroes at work. There were seldom more than two or three working together on one farm. This puzzled the boy. But it was not until they had been traveling through the country for some time that he spoke of it.

"I thought there were big plantations here with lots

of slaves," he remarked, turning to Mr. Perkins, who had settled down comfortably in his seat and was driving with the reins held loosely in one hand.

Mr. Perkins shook his head. "They don't call them slaves in this part of the country, David," he said. "They call them servants. And there aren't many large plantations in Missouri. There are good-sized farms mostly. There's a tobacco grower over in Greenfield, though, who has a big place. Man by the name of Cooper."

"Oh!" exclaimed David, taken completely by surprise. "That's where I'm going."

"So am I," said Mr. Perkins, as David caught his breath and thought guiltily that he must watch his tongue more carefully. "That's one of my stops. And here's another."

He turned his horse into a driveway which led to a shabby white house, half-hidden by trees. A little girl, who was rolling a hoop in front of the house, spied the wagon. She stared at it for a moment. Then she cried, "There's a peddler coming, Mama. There's a peddler coming," and ran around the house.

By the time Mr. Perkins and David had reached the end of the driveway near the back steps, three women, several small children, and a towheaded man with a pitchfork over his shoulder were waiting there to greet him. A tired-looking colored woman with a red bandanna on her head stood in the kitchen doorway with a baby in her arms.

Turning the gray mare and the wagon so that both

faced the road from which he had come, Mr. Perkins stood up and lifted his hat.

"Howdy, folks," he said, "pleasant day, ain't it? And here I am with things in my wagon that will tickle the fancy of each and every one of you: needles, pins, hooks, eyes, buttons, scissors, pretty yard goods for the ladies, spectacles if your eyesight's growing dim, dishes, brooms, tinware, toys for the little ones, and the finest horse liniment made in all the land. Step up. Step up and look things over, and tell me what you'll have."

Almost before Mr. Perkins had finished speaking, one of the women was examining a broom. Another asked to look at a pair of good sharp scissors, and a third lifted up the youngest child, who was clamoring to see what was inside the wagon. The man propped his pitchfork against the house and came closer to watch the proceedings.

The only person who did not move was the colored woman. She still stood in the doorway. If David had been looking at her, he might have noticed that she was staring at the peddler with a puzzled expression on her face. But the boy had no time to pay attention to any one person, for he suddenly found himself very busy helping Mr. Perkins display his wares. Before long a shiny tin dishpan, a dozen bone buttons, and a blue and white china pitcher had changed hands.

"And how about you, Auntie?" Mr. Perkins called out suddenly, looking over the heads of the others at the colored woman. "Nothing for you today?"

"Melinda don't need anything," one of the women said, looking surprised. "We keep her fixed with everything she wants."

"Oh, I'm sure of that, ma'am," Mr. Perkins said quickly. "But here's a bit of muslin might make her a nice kerchief for Sunday. There is a bad place in it here, so I can't sell it." He held up a piece of white muslin and pointed out a spot where the threads were pulled apart. "How about it, Melinda?" he asked. "It was woven way up north, and it's *free*. Do you understand me? It's *free!*"

"Free!" Melinda repeated, her eyes filling suddenly with tears, and a joyous expression coming into her face. "Yes sir, I understands you. But I don't need nothin', like my mistress said, though I thank you just the same." Putting her hand over her mouth, she turned quickly and went into the house.

Mr. Perkins shrugged his shoulders. "Too bad," he said. "I figured maybe she could use it. Well, folks, if that's all I can sell you today, I reckon we'd better be getting on."

He put a box back in place, asked David to move the basket of chinaware to a spot toward the middle of the wagon where it wouldn't rattle, and sat down in the driver's seat. No sooner had he picked up the reins, however, than the towheaded man, who had not yet spoken a word, laid a hand on the horse's bridle.

"Just a minute, Mr. Peddler," he drawled, wrinkling his brows and looking hard at Simon Perkins. "There's something about you that is mighty familiar to me, and I can't rightly figure it out. Seems like I've seen you around here before. A couple of months ago it was, maybe — before Melinda's boy ran off to the North."

Mr. Perkins shook his head, and his hands tightened on the reins. "Reckon not, friend," he said to the man who was still staring at him. "I ain't been peddlin' 'round in these parts before. Get up, Nell! Get up!"

He flicked the reins, and the horse started up so suddenly that the towheaded man lost his hold on the bridle and was left standing in the middle of the road, staring after the wagon with his mouth open. Looking back, David saw him scratch his head thoughtfully and pick up his pitchfork.

"Is he coming after us?" Mr. Perkins asked, as he turned the horse onto the highway.

"No sir, he's just standing there talking to those women," David replied. Then, in a perplexed tone, he added, "Jingoes, you started up in a hurry. What was the matter?"

If Mr. Perkins heard this question, he certainly did not intend to answer it. Still gripping the reins tightly, all he said was, "Get up, Nell!" He did not speak again until they had traveled half a mile or more. Then, settling back in his seat, he drew a deep breath and turned to David, who was still wondering what had occurred to cause the peddler to leave his customers so speedily.

"I want to get as far as Saxton's Hollow, on the other side of the Missouri, before sundown," Mr. Perkins said, as if to explain his haste. "We'll spend the night there with my sister. There's not much use trying to peddle anything between here and there. Most folks in these parts can get to St. Louis to buy what they want." He loosened his hold on the reins and let Nell slow down to a walk. "I'm hungry. There's a bag of apples under one end of the seat. Don't you want one?" he asked.

"Yes sir," David replied promptly. The morning had been so busy, and he had eaten such a large breakfast at Lacey's Eating House, that he had not thought to buy dinner before he met the peddler. So for a long time he had been wondering how soon they would be getting some supper.

Fishing under the seat, he found the sack of fruit and selected two of the biggest apples. He passed one to Mr. Perkins and took a large bite out of the other.

"Makes me wish I had a big slab of one of Ma's apple pies," he said as soon as he could talk. And he began to tell the peddler about his mother's bakeshop. Then he told about Nancy and his brothers, and all about the day Mr. Lincoln was nominated and Robbie fell into the water.

He even told how he and Jim had rescued the younger boy. But when Mr. Perkins asked, "Who's Jim?" David answered, "Oh just a friend of mine," and stopped talking. The peddler, too, was silent. And the two rode on together, each busy with his own thoughts.

They traveled through a sleepy little town where the children were just coming out of school. They waited while a farmer's boy drove a herd of cows across the road. They rattled over a wooden bridge which spanned a winding creek.

They crossed the muddy-colored Missouri River on a little ferry and jogged on, up hill and down, past more farms large and small. At last, when the sun was low in the sky, Mr. Perkins turned Nell into a narrow lane and stopped before a low brick house.

"Here's where we'll spend the night, if we're lucky," he said to David. "Jump down, boy, and see if anyone's home."

Delighted to stretch his legs, which were stiff from riding so long, David jumped to the ground and rapped on the front door. It was opened in a moment by a pleasant-faced, gray-haired woman with a pair of spectacles pushed up on her forehead and a half-knitted sock in one hand.

"What is it, boy?" she asked when she saw David. "What do you want?"

"He wants to know if you can feed two hungry travelers and give them beds for the night," Simon Perkins called in a queer cracked voice. "How about it, ma'am? Can you take us in?"

The woman shook her head. "I'm real sorry," she said. "This isn't an inn. You'll find a good one on the road just beyond — " She hesitated a minute. Then, pulling her spectacles down on her nose, she stared at the peddler, who had clambered from his seat and was coming up the low steps.

"Simon!" she exclaimed softly, holding the door open so that the peddler and David could enter the house. "That beard! What will you do next? And with your hair so untidy, I — I didn't know you at first."

"Good!" said Simon Perkins with a chuckle. "I hoped you wouldn't, Mary. It means Hasler and I have done a fine job. I'll tell you all about it later. Is your good husband at home?"

"No," the woman replied, leading the way into a comfortably furnished living room with white curtains at the windows and two well-worn armchairs before the fireplace. "He's gone to Jefferson City, and he won't be back till next week. Susie is in the kitchen, but there's no one else in the house."

She looked at the peddler and shook her head despairingly. "Oh, Simon," she wailed, "you'll land in jail before this is all over. Who is this boy you have with you?"

"He's all right," Simon Perkins declared, seeming for the first time since they had entered the house to remember David. "He comes from Chicago, he's going with me as far as Greenfield, and his name is David Morgan."

He turned to David who was just behind him. "This is my sister, Mrs. Carroll, lad," he said. "I haven't seen her in some time and we've a lot to talk over. Do you know anything about horses?"

"Yes, sir," David answered, leaning over to stroke the ears of a fat old spaniel which was sniffing at his legs. "I used to help my friend Mr. Adams take care of horses at the Tremont House stable sometimes."

"Then please take Nell to the barn at the back of the

house and look after her for me, will you?" Mr. Perkins asked, sinking wearily into the nearest arm chair and beginning to unfasten the strings which held his beard in place. "You'll have no trouble finding feed and water. Put the wagon in the barn, but don't touch anything in it. Leave it just as it is. And come back here as soon as you've finished."

David nodded. He did not want to leave the room, for he was just as curious about Mr. Perkins' beard as Mrs. Carroll seemed to be. It was disappointing to be sent away just when it looked as though he might find out something about it. However, there was nothing he could do but go, and he started reluctantly for the barn.

As he unhitched the traces, removed the heavy harness, and threw a halter over Nell's neck a few moments later, all sorts of questions were chasing around in his mind. Who was this Mr. Perkins who dressed like a peddler but didn't speak or act like one most of the time? What was the business he was in, which he called a good business, but which was dangerous and strange? Why had he been afraid that he was being followed when he left the only farmhouse at which they had stopped that afternoon? And what had Mrs. Carroll meant when she talked about his landing in jail?

Each question was like a piece in a puzzle, David thought. If he could only fit them all together, he might have the answers. But other questions were bothering him, too, as he put Nell into a stall and filled the feed box with oats.

He was becoming more worried and uncertain every hour about what he should do when he reached Greenfield, and how he should find Jim. It had been all very fine, when he was safe at home in Chicago, to talk so bravely about helping his friend. But without Uncle Carl to help him, and with no one to whom he could turn for advice, he was almost beginning to wish he hadn't been quite so brave.

"Well, fretting about it won't help any," he told himself at last. "I'll just have to wait till I get to Greenfield and see what happens then." He patted Nell's neck and looked around the barn to make sure that he had left everything in order. Then he started outdoors. At the threshold of the barn, however, he remembered that his carpetbag was still in the wagon.

"I'll need it tonight," he thought, and turning back, he climbed up and felt around under the seat for the bag. During the journey, it had slid almost to the other side of the wagon. Leaning over the wheel, David stuck his head under the seat and tried in vain to reach the bag.

Suddenly he felt a strong hand grab him by the seat of his pantaloons, and a voice snapped angrily, "What are you doing in that wagon?"

David raised his head so quickly that he hit it a sharp crack on the wagon seat. Jumping to the barn floor, he rubbed the bump as he looked at Mr. Perkins. "I was just getting my carpetbag," he explained unhappily.

Mr. Perkins sighed. "I'm sorry David," he said

apologetically. "I ask you to trust me, and then I'm suspicious of you. Go on, boy, get your bag and take it in the house. Then please come back here and give me a hand with a box which I have here in the wagon and want to take inside. And forgive me for jumping on you that way, will you?"

"Yes sir," said David. His head hurt. He had been so taken by surprise that his heart was thumping like a steam engine. But Mr. Perkins did really look so sorry that the boy couldn't help smiling at him. Scrambling into the wagon again, David found his bag, took it to the house, and set it just inside the front door. Then, still rubbing his head, he went back to the barn.

Mr. Perkins was waiting there for him. A long, narrow, flat, wooden box with a hinged top lay at his feet. David stared at the box curiously. If it had come out of the wagon, he couldn't imagine where it had been kept, for he had not seen it among the other boxes and baskets that afternoon.

"It's not heavy. It's just awkward to carry," Mr. Perkins explained. "You take that end and I'll take this."

David picked up his end, and carrying the box between them, he and Mr. Perkins walked toward the back of the house.

"Look out," warned Simon Perkins, as they started through the open door which led into the kitchen. "Better go in backward, David. Be careful, there. Don't tip it. One of the hinges is broken, and the clasp came loose just before I left St. Louis. It must be fixed before we go on tomorrow, and — ouch!"

Stubbing his toe on the low step at the threshold of the room, Mr. Perkins lost his balance and his hold on the box at the same instant. With a thud, his end of the box dropped to the kitchen floor. The lid fell back, and out on the floor tumbled the strangest assortment of things David had ever seen in his life. Gray wigs, bonnets, gloves, false beards, long skirts, pantaloons, and black mustaches were all jumbled together. And dozens of small metal compasses were rolling across the room in every direction.

Susie, a jolly-looking, black-skinned woman who stood at the stove stirring something in a pot, turned around quickly and surveyed the wreckage. "I declare, Master Simon!" she exclaimed, laying down her spoon. "What a mess!" She got down on her knees with a grunt and began to gather the things together, dumping them into the box again in an untidy heap. Mr. Perkins sat down on the nearest chair and rubbed his toe.

"Confound that step!" he muttered. "I always forget it's there." He smiled wryly at David, who was squatting on his heels with a compass in his hand and his brows drawn together in a puzzled frown. "Well, lad," he said, "I reckon there's no use trying to hide my business from you any longer. You know now what I'm up to, don't you?"

David did not reply at once. Staring at the compass, he watched its needle swing slowly back and forth until it settled, pointing to the north. Then the pieces of the puzzle, which he had been trying to fit together in his mind while he worked in the barn, suddenly fell into place.

"Yes!" he exclaimed softly, looking at Mr. Perkins with shining eyes, "you're — you're helping slaves escape. Giving them compasses to show them the way north, and clothes that will change the way they look, and —" He hesitated. Then he added, in a perplexed tone, "But you said you were born down south."

"He sure was," Susie announced, without giving Mr. Perkins time to speak. "An' his pappy owned a mess of slaves. When he died —" Susie got slowly to her feet and smoothed down her apron. "When he died," she repeated, "Master Simon set 'em all free — even me. I works here now, and I gets good wages, and I likes the freedom. But since Miz Carroll and Master Simon always makes me feel like this is my own home, too, I knows I'm welcome to stay. Ain't that right, Miz Carroll?" She beamed at Mrs. Carroll, who had come to the door on hearing the noise in the kitchen.

"It certainly is, Susie," Mrs. Carroll replied. "You're one of the best friends we've ever had." Picking up a wig which lay near her feet, she folded it neatly and put it in the box. Then she crossed the room and peered into the pot on the stove. "Is there enough chicken stew here for everybody?" she asked.

Susie chuckled. " 'Deed there is, ma'am," she declared. "I had a feelin' we'd be havin' company, an' I done made plenty. Reckon I'd better fix some biscuits, though. That boy crawlin' around on the floor after them compasses looks like he could eat a dozen."

David grinned. "I guess I could," he said.

And he almost did just that! Never did any meal taste better to David than the supper he ate that night, sitting at the table in the dining room with Mr. Perkins at one end and Mrs. Carroll at the other, and with Susie passing dishes filled with steaming food which smelled as good as it tasted. It was a meal he would never forget — not only because of what he ate, but because of what he learned.

Now that Mr. Perkins' secret had been discovered, that gentleman was ready to tell David almost everything the boy wanted to know. But David asked so many questions so rapidly that at last Simon Perkins insisted upon telling his story in his own way.

"You see, David," he said, in his slow, soft voice, "I've been in this work for a good many years. I *hate* slavery. I've hated it ever since I was fourteen years old, when my father needed some money and had to sell a boy named George to a hard-faced slave buyer from Louisiana." Mr. Perkins paused, helped himself to the chicken stew which Susie was passing for the second time, and took a good-sized mouthful.

"George was my friend," he went on as soon as he could speak. "We'd grown up together, played together, learned to swim together, fished together, and done all the things boys like to do. And then George was sold. His mother cried for three days and —"

"And poor Simon wouldn't speak to anyone for a

week," Mrs. Carroll put in.

"Didn't want to," Mr. Perkins said. "The whole business made me feel sick all over. I made up my mind then that I'd fight slavery all my life. I've done it, too, in every way I know how."

"And worried me to death, during all these years," Mrs. Carroll added, handing David some grape jelly to put on his hot biscuit. "He'll end in jail, David, or have to move up north if he isn't careful. I know he will."

Mr. Perkins chuckled. "I've been in some tight spots, all right," he admitted. "Had to leave Mississippi finally, so I came up the river to Missouri, where my sister and her husband had built this little house.

"Then I decided that I was growing old and that the safest way for me to get a chance to talk to slaves, and to slip them compasses, or clothes, or information about people who would help them, was for me to be a traveling preacher or a peddler. So I've been both — sometimes with a beard, sometimes with a long mustache, and sometimes with no trimmings at all.

He grinned at David. "It was the preacher you talked with this morning," he explained, "and I thought you'd ride with the preacher in his carriage this afternoon. But I heard someone was spreading the word around St. Louis that four slaves who escaped the other day had been seen talking to a smooth-faced old parson in a black coat. So I changed my plans and my appearance, with Mr. Hasler's help."

"Is Mr. Hasler working for it, too?" David asked,

leaning both elbows on the table and looking intently at Mr. Perkins.

"For what?" Mr. Perkins wanted to know.

"For the Underground Railroad!" David exclaimed. "I know about it. Oh, Mr. Perkins, will you tell me what to do about Jim?" And without waiting for an answer, David launched into the story of Jim and Jim's freedom paper and Mr. Snively.

By the time he had finished, Susie had taken the plates away and had brought in a raisin and apple pudding. And by the time the pudding had disappeared, Mr. Perkins had promised to help David get in touch with Jim, and to tell both boys the best way to get out of Missouri and into Illinois.

"Now," said Mr. Perkins, as he folded his napkin and pushed back his chair, "we'll mend the box that's in the kitchen. Then we'll have a little visit with my sister and get to bed. I am anxious to leave this neighborhood tomorrow, before daylight."

So David and Mr. Perkins fixed the broken hinge and the clasp on the long, flat box, and Mrs. Carroll repacked it neatly with the things which had tumbled out. Then, while Susie lighted their way with a lantern, the boy and the man carried the box to the barn and set it on the floor.

David was still wondering where it had come from. He watched curiously while Simon Perkins stepped up to one side of the wagon and slid his fingers between two of the planks. Like the hinged cover on Grandfather Morgan's desk at home in Chicago, the bottom plank along the side opened out.

David whistled softly under his breath. "It's a false bottom, isn't it?" he asked in amazement.

"That's right," Mr. Perkins agreed. "There's just enough space in there for a man to lie flat on his stomach, and then for this box to fit in beside him," he explained. "Want to crawl in and try it?"

David nodded, too excited to speak. Hoisting himself up, he wriggled into the compartment under the false bottom of the wagon. It was dark and stuffy, and so shallow that he could barely turn his head from one side to the other. Wondering how anyone could bear to travel in such close, cramped quarters, he crawled out again and took a deep breath of fresh air.

"Will Jim have to ride in there?" he asked, wrinkling his nose in disgust.

"Can't tell yet just how we'll get Jim away," Mr. Perkins replied, motioning to David to help him put the narrow box in its place. "It's not the most comfortable way in the world to travel, but I've carried lots of people in this wagon. I reckon when folks are headed for a free land, they don't care much how they get there."

He put up the side of the wagon and made sure that it was securely fastened. Then he and David followed Susie's bobbing lantern to the house. The next morning before sunrise they were on their way to Greenfield.

chapter *11*

Plans for Escape

S OMEWHERE in the village of Greenfield a clock
struck slowly six times. David sat on a fallen tree,
with his cap pulled down over his ears and his hands
deep in the pockets of his heavy jacket. He was waiting for Simon Perkins, who had left him at the out-
skirts of the village and driven off alone down the road
which led to Mr. Cooper's tobacco farm.

"It will be too risky to take you right to the farm,"
Mr. Perkins had explained to David that noon, as
they stopped by the roadside to eat the lunch which
Susie and Mrs. Carroll had put up for them. "Jim
might call out your name if he saw you, and that would
get us all into trouble, sure as shooting."

"But how will you know which boy is Jim?" David

had asked, in a worried voice, tossing away a chicken leg which he had gnawed clean.

"Oh, I'll find Jim all right, if he's around," Mr. Perkins had replied. "I may not have much time to talk to him, though. You say he can read pretty well. Perhaps you'd better write out a message that I can slip to him."

Fishing in his pocket, Mr. Perkins had pulled out a stubby pencil and a piece of paper, and handed them both to David.

"Tell Jim to come to the empty barn near the burned-out house just beyond the white church, after dark on the first night he can get away," he said. "Tell him you'll wait for him in the barn every night till he comes."

"But suppose he doesn't come for a week or so!" David had exclaimed. "Where shall I stay in the day-time?"

"At Bartlett's Inn in the village," Mr. Perkins had replied. "Tim Bartlett's a friend of mine. He'll look out for you till Jim shows up, and start you both on your way home if I leave before then. Go on, lad, write down what I've told you, and warn Jim to tear the message up as soon as he's read it. Then we'll get along."

So David had written down Mr. Perkins' directions and scrawled underneath them a line, telling Jim that he had his freedom paper. Then he had signed his name to the message and handed it to the old man. All that had been five hours earlier. And for the last two of those five hours David had been waiting anxiously for Simon Perkins to return from the tobacco farm with news of Jim. At the same time he had been thinking about the journey he and Mr. Perkins had made that day.

Since they had wanted to reach Greenfield before dark, they had stopped at only a few farmhouses, and the peddler had sold little from his supply of tinware and drygoods. Nevertheless, Mr. Perkins was pleased with his day's work, for at one place he had been able to slip a compass into a gnarled brown hand. And at a trim gray farmhouse farther on, he had managed to tell a frightened girl where to go for help when she was ready to run away from her owner — a heavyset Negro, who, during the whispered conversation, had been unsuspectingly trying on a pair of spectacles.

It had never before occurred to David, whose sharp eyes had seen all that was going on, that there were Negro slaveowners as well as Negro slaves. This had seemed very strange indeed, and he had said so to Simon Perkins as they drove away from the gray house.

"Nothing strange about it!" Mr. Perkins had replied, urging Nell to a trot. "You didn't think all slaves in the world were dark-skinned and all masters white, did you? Not by a long shot, lad! The color of a man's skin hasn't anything to do with whether he owns slaves or not. It's the way he thinks."

"Then," David had begun, "why —"

But Mr. Perkins had gone on speaking, as though he hadn't heard him. "There've been slaves and slaveowners in different parts of the world for thousands of years," he had continued. "I reckon there always will be, too, until all men learn to be decent to each other. But we're learning fast here in America, David. Somehow we're going to get rid of slavery here, and fix it so that every person in this land can stand up proudly and say, 'I'm free!'"

It was just as Mr. Perkins had said "free," David remembered, that they had rounded the top of a hill and come upon a farmer's boy with a big flock of sheep. Simon Perkins had had to pull Nell to the side of the road to let the bleating animals pass. And by the time the wagon had started up again, the peddler had begun to tell David about some of the trouble he had run into while helping slaves escape.

"I'll bet Mr. Perkins is in some kind of trouble this very minute — he's been gone so long. Glory! I wish he'd come back," David thought uneasily.

Reaching down for a stone, he shied it halfheartedly in the direction of a squirrel which was chattering in a nearby tree. With a flick of its tail, the little creature darted off, scolding sharply. Two crows cawed shrilly overhead. A cold breeze rustled the tall stalks of dry golden rod, and the sun slipped slowly behind the horizon. David shivered and stood up.

"I'm going to find out what's wrong," he said aloud, and started toward the road down which Mr. Perkins and the wagon had disappeared sometime earlier.

All at once the boy stopped, stood still, and listened. Then he began to run. From around a bend in the road he had heard the clip-clop of a horse's hoofs and the faint sound of tin hitting against tin. He was breathless when he reached the peddler's wagon.

"Did you — did you find him?" he asked eagerly, as Mr. Perkins pulled Nell to a stop. "Are you all right? Did you find Jim?"

Simon Perkins nodded. "Found him right off and had a talk with him, too," he said, when David had climbed over the wheel. As Nell started up again, the old man chuckled.

"Reckon you didn't know we had some wagon spokes loose, did you, lad?" he asked. "That's because they weren't loose when I left you. But by the time I had reached Cooper's farm I'd fixed it so that they were so loose I had to have a couple of boys help me tighten them up. And I saw to it that one of those boys was Jim."

"How is he?" David asked, looking admiringly at Mr. Perkins. "Is he all right?"

"He's fine," Mr. Perkins replied. "But he's scared. Or at least he was until I talked to him. It seems that since the day Mark and Dora ran off, Mr. Cooper has lost two other slaves. He's been threatening to move his family and all his people down to Texas, and Jim found out today that he's all set to start south next week."

"Looks as if we'd come just in time," David remarked, rubbing some dust from his eyes.

"That's right," agreed Mr. Perkins. "Jim's going to try to get away tonight."

"Tonight!" echoed David joyfully. "Will he come to the barn?"

Mr. Perkins nodded. "You and I will go to the inn now, though, so that you can get the lay of the land," he said. "Look!" He pointed ahead with a bony finger. "We'll be passing the barn in a minute. There it is, in the middle of that field. Mark it well, for you'll have to come back here alone."

"Is there a lane leading to it?" David asked, peering through the dusk at the shadowy building which stood back some distance from the highway.

"Right here," Simon Perkins replied, pulling Nell up for a moment. "It's pretty well overgrown with weeds, but you can find it if you look sharp. Or you can cut across the fields.

"Now, listen. After we get to Tim's and arrange for him to help us, you come back here. When Jim comes, wait right in the barn with him till you hear the courthouse clock strike eleven. Then bring him straight to the inn, making sure that no one sees you. Knock three times on the back window — that's a signal for the Underground — and hide in the shadows until I let you in. Then you'll have nothing to worry about till tomorrow."

"Yes sir," David said.

Little shivers of excitement were running up and down his spine as he thought of coming back to the deserted-looking barn after nightfall. And his heart was pounding with excitement when he slipped through the gaping barn door two hours later. Holding his breath, he stood motionless for an instant, wondering if perhaps Jim had come there before him and were hiding in the shadows.

"Jim!" he called softly. "Jim, are you there?"

No answer came to his whispered question except a rustling noise in the hay heaped in one corner of the barn and the scratching sound of scurrying little feet. David jumped. Then he grinned at himself in the dark.

"It's nothing but rats," he thought with relief. Groping his way to the side of the barn, he sat down on the floor with his back against the wall and prepared to wait for Jim.

It was a blustery, windy night. Clouds scurried across the moon, so that the long fingers of light which streamed through the cracks of the ramshackle barn came and went fitfully. Overhead the rafters creaked. And dry leaves which had drifted through the open door made faint swishing sounds as they blew around the floor in gusty whirlpools. Outside and in, the world was filled with noises which seemed strange and a little frightening to a boy who had grown up with the sounds of a city in his ears.

David almost wished that he were safe at home, or back in the snug little room in Bartlett's Inn, where he and Simon Perkins had eaten a good hot supper soon after their arrival. But even more strongly, he wished that Jim would come. And all at once his wish came true.

Suddenly, without a sound, a slim, dark figure

slipped into the barn and stepped silently into a shadowy corner.

"Jim?" David asked softly, scrambling to his feet.

There was an instant's silence, then a low chuckle in the darkness. "You, Davy!" Jim whispered, stepping forward and grabbing David by both arms. "Jumpin' like you always do before you're sure. S'pose it hadn't been me?"

"But it was!" David exclaimed happily. "Oh Jim! Did you get away all right?"

"I'm here, ain't I?" Jim replied softly. "An' nobody knows it yet but you an' me. Sneaked off as soon as it was dark and hid in the bushes till I figured it was safe to come across the fields. Crawled most of the way, like a snake, so's nobody'd see me. I declare I wish the wind would blow out that dratted moon." He looked around uneasily. "Where are we going now?" he asked.

"Nowhere till eleven o'clock," David answered, in a low tone. "We might as well sit down." He squatted down again on the floor, pulling Jim after him. "Mr. Perkins figures that by eleven folks will be abed and it will be safe for us to go to the inn, where he's waiting for us," he added.

Jim sighed. "I'd sure like to get as far away as I can as soon as I can," he whispered. "Come morning Mr. Cooper will find out I've gone and chase after me. Have you got my freedom paper?"

"Uh-huh!" David reached inside his jacket. Then he remembered that Nancy had sewn his pocket shut.

"Wait till we get to the inn," he said. "I can't get at it now. But it's safe, and I have your money, too."

Jim drew a deep breath. "Once I get my hands on that paper, I'll sure feel better," he declared, still speaking in a whisper. "How did you find out I was here in Greenfield? Did Mark tell you?"

"Uh-huh," David said again. "He and Dora. They went on to Canada all right."

"Me too," Jim announced, pulling his knees up under his chin. "I'm goin' to Canada as fast as I can. There won't be no Snivelys there."

"What did that old devil do to you?" David asked, moving around in the dark till he sat closer to Jim.

"Tricked me," Jim replied shortly. "Came asneakin' into my little house and told me your mammy was sick, and I must get dressed and go for a doctor. Soon as I stepped outside, he and another man grabbed me and stuffed my mouth with rags. Then they tied me up. No matter how hard I fought 'em, there weren't nothin' I could do."

He shivered a little and pulled his jacket closer around him.

"Then what?" prompted David.

"Reckon you know then what," Jim answered in an undertone. "I don't like to talk about it. Of course, Mr. Cooper's all right. Treats his people fair, don't often work 'em too hard, and feeds 'em pretty good. But I'd rather work till I couldn't stand up and eat nothin' but flies, and be free."

"That old Snively," David muttered. "I'd like to —"

"Sh!" Jim warned, suddenly sitting bolt upright and grabbing David by the arm, "What's that?"

"Just rats," David said, "over there in the hay."

Jim laughed softly. "Looks like I've got the fidgets," he apologized. "I'll be glad when we get out of here. Tell me what you all have been doin' since I came away."

So, speaking very low, David told Jim about some of the things that had happened during the summer, and the two boys whispered together until the courthouse clock boomed solemnly eleven times. Then David scrambled to his feet.

"Come on," he commanded. "It's not far." Crouching low, he started to run across the field. Jim followed him.

Clouds now hid the moon completely. There was enough light, however, so that the boys had no trouble in finding and following the road. In silence they hurried on past darkened houses. Once a dog ran out at them, barking loudly. But David stood still and spoke to him in a friendly voice. And after a minute he wagged his tail and trotted back to where he had come from.

The boys met no one, even after they had reached the center of the little town. Except for two lighted windows on the second floor, Bartlett's Inn looked shut up for the night. David led the way down the narrow alley between the inn and the grocery store next door.

"Stay here in the shadows," he whispered to Jim.

With his heart beating fast, he stepped up to one of the back windows and knocked gently on the glass three times. Then he waited, his eyes on the back door. Slowly and quietly the door opened. Without a sound, the two boys slipped inside.

"Made it without a hitch," Simon Perkins' voice said softly in the dark. "Good boys! Stand still till I make a light." He struck a lucifer match on the wall and touched it to the candle which he had in his hand.

"Come on," he whispered, and tiptoed up a narrow flight of stairs and into a little back bedroom. When he and the boys were safely inside the room, Mr. Perkins shut and bolted the door. Then he turned to Jim. "Still scared?" he asked.

"Not now, mister," Jim replied with a slow grin. "The thing that had me scared most was thinkin' about being carried clear to Texas."

Simon Perkins nodded. "I know," he said, setting the candle down on a table. "Well, if my plans work out right, you'll soon be far away from Mr. Cooper. Sit down and get your breath. Then we'll try some things on you."

"What things?" Jim asked, perching himself on the edge of a straight-backed chair and looking hastily around the room.

"These," Mr. Perkins replied. He opened a door to a corner cupboard and took out a high-necked black dress, a black cape, and a heavy black veil. "Hung 'em up so I'd get the wrinkles out of them," he remarked, holding the clothes out to Jim. "Here, see if they fit."

"Fit *me?*" Jim asked, opening his eyes wide in amazement. "Mister, I can't wear women's clothes."

"Nonsense!" Simon Perkins exclaimed impatiently. "You told me this afternoon you'd do anything you had to do to get your freedom. Now stand up, lad. Take off your jacket and try on this dress."

Jim swallowed hard and stood up meekly.

David grinned and smothered a giggle when Mr. Perkins had fastened the dress, put the cape over Jim's shoulders, and set the bonnet on his head with the heavy veil hiding his face. "Glory, Jim!" David exclaimed. "You look like a —"

"He looks fine!" Mr. Perkins interrupted. "All he needs is these gloves." He handed Jim a pair of black cotton gloves. "Put them on," he urged. "That's right. Now walk to the door and back."

"Can't," Jim protested behind the veil. "My feet'll get all tangled up in —"

"Go on," Mr. Perkins insisted. "Try."

Stumbling a little, Jim slowly made his way to the door and back.

"Reckon I'd better try again," he said, seeing a dissatisfied look on Simon Perkins' face.

So he tried again and again and again, until at last Simon Perkins said, "You're getting the hang of it all right, Jim. Now practice sitting down and standing up."

"Can I take this hanging thing off first?" Jim asked in a muffled tone, pointing to the veil. "It don't let me breathe."

Simon Perkins shook his head. "You'll have to get used to it," he said, "but if your luck holds, you'll only have to wear it half a day."

Jim pushed the veil up just enough to draw a deep breath. Then he began to practice sitting down in the straight-backed chair and standing up again, without falling over his skirt.

At last Simon Perkins declared, "You'll do. Take the things off, lad."

With a sigh of relief, the boy removed his disguise and helped David hang the clothing on a nail in the cupboard. Then, while the two boys sat side by side on the low bed and the spluttering candle threw strange shadows on the wall behind them, Simon Perkins unfolded his plan for Jim's escape.

"There's a stagecoach leaving tomorrow morning at six o'clock for a place called Fullerton," he told the boys. "It stops in front of the inn to pick up passengers. Tim will knock on your door, tell you when to come down, and see that you get aboard."

"Can we get on together?" asked David.

Simon Perkins nodded. "You'll have to pretend that Jim is your mother or your aunt or your older sister," he explained. "You two can talk it over later and decide which would be the easiest. But remember, once you have decided, you mustn't forget your story for one second.

"Jim, never lift that veil for an instant. Keep your cape around you and both gloves on all the time. And don't talk at all if you can help it."

"I won't," Jim promised. "I reckon I'll be too scared to say a word, anyway."

"Well, try not to let anyone know you're scared," Mr. Perkins advised him. "Let David take care of the fare and answer any questions. Fortunately the trip is not long. Tim tells me that the only passengers leaving from here are a Mr. and Mrs. Johnson and their sick baby. Likely they'll be so busy looking after their child, they'll pay little heed to you."

David leaned forward, his hands clasped around his knees and his brows drawn together in a frown. "What I want to know is what we do when we get to Fullerton," he said.

"Leave the stage and walk down the road to your right until you come to a small white house with green shutters and two chimneys," Mr. Perkins replied. "It's the only white house on that road, and you can't miss it. Of course, you'll feel like hurrying, but don't. Walk slowly, and be careful every minute not to do anything that will make people look at you."

David nodded, and Jim stared, round-eyed, at Mr. Perkins.

"When you get to the house," Simon Perkins continued, "knock on the door. Say to the woman who answers, 'Tim Bartlett says to pass us on.' She'll hide you both until it's safe to send you on your way."

"Will we have to pay her?" Jim asked.

"No!" David replied quickly, speaking up before Mr. Perkins had time to answer. "It's the Underground Railroad, Jim. That's the way it works."

"That's right," agreed Simon Perkins, crossing one knee over the other. "It's the Underground all right, and everyone who travels on it, as well as everyone who runs it, is in great danger most of the time."

He glanced soberly from one boy to the other. "It will be punishment and slavery again for Jim if he's captured, and five years in jail for you or anyone else in Missouri who is caught helping him, David. That's a good thing to keep in mind."

"Yes sir," David said soberly.

Jim moved restlessly and laid a hand on the other boy's knee. "I don't want to get no one in trouble," he protested to Mr. Perkins. "Leastwise Davy. He's brought me my freedom paper and my money, and now I can get on to Canada alone. I —"

David broke in impatiently. "Oh, hush up, Jim!" he exclaimed. "If you think I'm going north one way and you another, you're just plain crazy. We're going to stick together till we get to Chicago, no matter what happens."

A slow smile spread over Jim's face, and his fingers tightened on David's knee. Mr. Perkins stood up.

"Better do some more practicing tonight with that skirt and bonnet, Jim," he advised. "I'm off to bed. And since I won't dare see you in the morning, we'd better say good-by now."

"Are you leaving before we do?" David asked, getting to his feet.

Simon Perkins shook his head. "No, I'll stay around here for a day or so," he said. "If I left in the morning,

I'd surely be suspected of helping Jim get away. But if I stay —" He hesitated, and there was a twinkle in his blue eyes. "If I stay," he repeated, "maybe I can help Mr. Cooper look for his runaway along another road than the one that goes to Fullerton."

He held out his hand, first to Jim and next to David. "Good luck, lads," he said. "Watch four ways at once, and keep your wits about you. If you get into trouble, run like blazes or fight like wild Indians. I've an idea you'll make it all right."

"If we do, it will be because you've given us so much help," David declared, feeling suddenly that he was taking leave of an old friend. "Jingoes, Mr. Perkins, you've been — if you hadn't — I mean —" He grinned slowly, hanging on all the time to Simon Perkins' hand. "I guess I'm just trying to say 'Thank you,'" he blurted out at last.

The old man patted his shoulder. "Say it in a letter after you and Jim get safely home," he told the boy, as he slipped back the bolt on the door. "You can send it to me at my sister's in Saxton's Hollow."

"I will," David promised. "I —" But Simon Perkins had disappeared through the half-open door and pulled it softly shut behind him.

chapter *12*

Discovered!

THE STAGECOACH which made the trip three times a week between Greenfield and Fullerton was an ancient, ramshackle, dirty affair. But neither the dirt nor the rickety condition of the vehicle bothered Jim. With his black-gloved hands folded tightly in his lap, he sat close to David in the corner where Tim Bartlett had put him several hours earlier.

Even with the cape pulled tightly around his shoulders, he was cold, and the heavy veil which hid his face still seemed stifling. However, although he was uncomfortable, and worried about what would happen when he and David reached Fullerton, he was happy.

His freedom paper was securely pinned to his undershirt. His money was safely tucked in his trousers pocket. Every turn of the wheel was taking him farther north, and so far none of his fellow travelers had seemed the least suspicious of his disguise.

As Simon Perkins had predicted, the Johnsons, who had taken the seat opposite David and Jim before the stage left Bartlett's Inn, were too busy with their sick baby to pay much heed to anyone else. There were just two other passengers. One was a red-faced farmer bound only for the next village, who had chosen to ride on top of the coach with the driver. The other — a big, sandy-haired man with a wart on his nose — had crowded into the seat beside David when the stage had stopped, ten miles beyond Greenfield, to pick up passengers and change horses.

David had feared, at first, that the big man was going to be quite talkative and ask questions which would be difficult to answer. But hardly had the stage started up again when the sick baby had begun to cry so loudly that for some time conversation had been impossible.

Now, however, the child had fallen asleep in the arms of his father — a stupid-looking, pudgy-faced young man. He and the big man with the wart on his nose had begun to discuss politics. And pretty little Mrs. Johnson was studying Jim with a worried look in her eyes. Leaning forward, she tapped the boy on his black-skirted knee.

"Do you feel all right, ma'am?" she asked in a kindly voice. "I've been watching you on and off for nearly an hour, and you've scarce moved. It's even hard to tell if you're beathing behind that heavy veil. Are you sick?"

Jim shook his head. "No'm," he said faintly. "I'm fine."

"She — she's all right, ma'am," David declared hastily. "It's just that — well, you know — when someone you love dies, you just don't like to talk."

Mrs. Johnson shook her head pityingly and sank back in her seat. "I know," she said. "It's dreadful hard to lose someone you care about." As though she were thinking at that moment of her baby, she turned and touched his cheek lightly.

The big man in the corner coughed behind his hand and fell over against David, as the lumbering coach lurched around a curve in the heavily rutted road.

"Good thing we have only a few more miles to ride," he said, righting himself. "This old rattletrap's going to fall apart before long."

David nodded uneasily and straightened his cap, which had fallen forward over one ear. Suddenly he noticed that Mr. Johnson was looking Jim up and down with a puzzled expression in his pale gray eyes. With a rush of dismay, David saw why.

In bracing himself against the swaying of the coach, Jim, who had managed so nicely up to this time, had forgotten at last to keep his feet hidden. Sticking out from under the hem of his neat black skirt was one heavy, mud-stained boot.

David's first impulse was to whisper to Jim to pull

his foot in. But he realized at once how foolish that would be. Trying to appear quite unconcerned, he bent over and pulled his carpetbag from under the seat, where he had placed it when the driver had announced that there was no room for small luggage on top of the stage. Leaning down, he opened the bag and fumbled inside, pretending to look for something. At the same time he shoved the satchel around so that it stood between Jim's feet and the prying eyes of Mr. Johnson.

Then, pulling out Abraham Lincoln's little gray dictionary, which was the first thing his hand had touched, he shut the bag. As he straightened up, he noticed that Mr. Johnson was whispering something behind his hand to his wife. She sent a long, slow look in Jim's direction, shook her head several times, and murmured in her husband's ear. Once more Mr. Johnson began to whisper, glancing sideways at Jim as he talked. This time when he had finished, his wife nodded hesitantly and took the baby from him.

David had caught only one word of the conversation: "reward." The boy's heart skipped a beat, but he whistled softly under his breath, as though there were nothing wrong. At the same time he was racking his brains to think of a way to warn Jim of his danger. Settling back in his seat, he slowly turned the pages of the gray book.

"You aren't fixing to read, are you?" the big man asked, looking at him in surprise.

David laughed nervously. "Well, I was," he replied,

closing the book and sticking it in the pocket of his
jacket. "But it seems like this coach is too jiggly."

Just then Mr. Johnson moved forward a little on the
opposite seat and smiled unpleasantly at David.

"You think you're a pretty smart young feller, don't
you?" he asked tauntingly. "But maybe not always
quite smart enough, eh?"

David flushed. "I don't think I know what you mean,
sir," he answered, moving a little closer to Jim.

"Oh, I reckon you do," Mr. Johnson said slowly.
"Reckon you know as well as I do that some black
veils hide more than sorrow. Wonder if this one does!"

Lunging forward suddenly, he yanked at Jim's veil
and ripped it from the bonnet. Like a streak of light-
ning, David sprang from his seat and landed on the
man, pounding him with his fists and kicking vigor-
ously at his legs.

"Get out, Jim!" David gasped. "Run for it! Run!"

With clenched fist, he landed a swift punch in Mr.
Johnson's right eye. Mrs. Johnson screamed and shrank
back in her corner. Wakened by the racket, the baby
began to howl. The big man struggled to his feet and
grabbed David by the shoulders, shouting all the time
at the driver to halt the coach, which was swaying
back and forth wildly.

David was still punching and kicking with all his
might. But Mr. Johnson managed finally to raise an
arm and deliver a hard blow on the boy's nose. Blood
streaming down his face, David stepped back. Just
then the driver, who had stopped his horses im-

mediately on hearing the commotion, pulled open the coach door.

"Run, Jim!" David panted, struggling in the grasp of the big man, who now had him firmly by the arm. "Quick! Run!"

But Jim did not even hear him, for he was no longer there. Somehow he had succeeded in opening the door on his side of the coach. With his skirts gathered around his waist and his bonnet bobbing up and down, he was streaking across the fields toward a big patch of woodland.

The driver, who had not yet missed his black-robed passenger, thrust his head inside the stagecoach. "What in tarnation's going on here?" he cried, yelling to make himself heard above the screaming baby. Then he saw David's face. "Jehoshaphat!" he exclaimed. "Who did that to you?"

"He did," David panted, wiping some blood from his chin. He pointed a gory finger at Mr. Johnson, who had one hand over a rapidly reddening eye, and was rubbing a bruised ankle with the other.

The stage driver grunted. "Looks like he's as bad off as you are. You must be quite a fighting cock," he said to David. "Well, get out of my coach afore you bloody it all up. We can settle this thing better on the road than in there, with that young'un howling its lungs out."

David sniffed and scrambled to his feet. Squirming out of the big man's grasp, he started to leave the coach by the door which Jim had left swinging open.

"Look out!" warned the big man sharply. "Don't let him get away!" He leaned forward suddenly to grab for David's jacket. So did Mr. Johnson on the opposite seat. With a crack, the two men's heads came together. The last thing David heard as he dashed for the woods, with both hands over his streaming nose, was a burst of violent swearing.

The boy did not stop to look back until he had crossed the fields and reached the shelter of the woodland. Then he turned his head and drew a deep shuddering sigh of relief. Apparently neither the big man nor Mr. Johnson had decided to set out immediately in pursuit of them, for there was no one running across the fields. The doors of the coach were closed, and the driver was climbing to his seat on top.

Panting heavily, David made his way a little deeper through the underbrush and into the woods. At last he sat down, with his back against a tree. He wiped his bloody hands on the ground and felt gingerly of his nose. Then he fished in a pocket of his pantaloons for a handkerchief. All at once he laughed weakly. Jim, with the black bonnet cocked over one ear, had stuck his head up cautiously from the center of a clump of bushes.

"You — you look as if you were — growing there," David gasped. "Come on out."

Jim's face was serious as he clambered out of the bushes, holding his skirts high. "Are you hurt bad?" he asked.

"Just my nose," David answered, taking the handkerchief away from his face. "It'll stop bleeding soon."

Jim leaned over him and shook his head. "I'm afraid it's goin' to puff big as a punkin." he declared. "But maybe not. You lay down there while I get myself out of this black thingamabob. Then we'd better make tracks."

"For where?" David asked, stretching out on the ground obediently and tipping his chin to the sky.

Jim yanked at the strings on his bonnet. "For a good hidin' place," he replied. "This spot's too close to the road. Maybe that Johnson man will come back here lookin' for us, or send someone after us. It ain't safe to stay here. We got to get away fast."

He unfastened the cape and dropped it to the ground. Then he began to fumble at the hooks on the back of the high-necked dress. At last, after a long struggle, he wriggled out of the garment, bunched it up under one arm, and picked up the cape and bonnet. "Feel like gettin' on yet?" he asked.

David sat up. "Yep," he said, with an attempt at a grin. "Bleeding's most stopped. What are you going to do with those things?"

"Take 'em," Jim replied shortly. "We'll need 'em, maybe." He held out his hand to help David to his feet. "Thank you," he said.

"For what?" David asked in surprise.

"For fightin' like a wildcat," Jim answered soberly. "I should have helped you, but lawsy, Dave, all I could think of right then was gettin' away."

"Lucky thing you did," David remarked. "You

couldn't fight in all those women's clothes anyway." He leaned down and picked up his cap from the ground. Then he looked at Jim in consternation.

"My carpetbag!" he exclaimed. "It's Ma's, really. I promised her I'd take good care of it and all the things she packed in it, too. And now —"

"Now it's on its way to Fullerton," Jim finished with a wry smile. "But they'd have caught you, sure, Dave, if you'd stopped to grab it. And the way things are turning out, you could never have lugged it all the way home. Your ma will understand."

David nodded. "I've still got Mr. Lincoln's dictionary, anyhow," he said, transferring the little gray book from his jacket pocket to the back pocket of his trousers for safekeeping. "Good thing I took it out of the bag when I did."

Jim agreed and glanced around fearfully. "Come on," he urged impatiently, "let's go."

Without even bothering to discuss it, both David and Jim knew that it would be extremely dangerous now to show their faces in Fullerton. Immediately after the arrival of the stagecoach, the story of their escape would be spread through the town. And more than one person would be eager to capture the runaway and hold him for the reward Jim's owner was sure to offer.

So the boys started off through the woods, using the little compass Mr. Perkins had given them and heading in a northeasterly direction away from the road. The country was hilly, rather rocky, and often covered with dense underbrush.

David's nose still smarted, and before long his head began to ache. Both boys were tired, since they had little rest the night before. Yet they pushed on without stopping until they had covered several miles and come upon a little creek. Then Jim dropped his bundle of clothing to the ground.

"Feel like I'm thirsty enough to swallow Lake Michigan," he declared, with an attempt at a grin. Kneeling down at the edge of the brook, he cupped his hands and drank deeply of the clear, cold water.

David squatted down beside him and drank too. He splashed the water up over his face, washing away the dried blood. Then he wet his handkerchief and tried to scrub the bloodstains from his jacket.

Jim perched himself on a rock close by, shook a stone out of his shoe, and looked around. "Where do you think we are, David?" he asked.

"Don't know," David replied. "Looks like our train on the Underground has run off its tracks, all right."

He squeezed the water out of his handkerchief and flapped it in the wind. "As I figure it, if we keep heading east from here, we'll run into the Mississippi, sure," he added. "Then all we have to do is to get across it somehow, and we'll be in Illinois. The rest —" He broke off suddenly. "Hey, Jim, you look terrible cold!" he exclaimed. "You'd better put that cape on."

"Don't want to," Jim said. "It'll just catch on the bushes and hold us back." He stood up and reached for the bundle of black clothes. "Come on, Dave. Let's get on our way again."

It seemed to David that they had rested hardly at all. But he scrambled reluctantly to his feet. Stepping carefully from stone to stone, the boys crossed the creek. Then, after a glance at the compass, they started off.

It was nearly dark when at last they reached the end of the woods and found themselves at the edge of a clearing. A road lay beyond the clearing. Between the woods and the road, not two hundred yards from where the boys were standing, was a shabby-looking farmhouse. Near the farmhouse were a good-sized barn and a hen house. A tall, thin woman, with her back to the boys, was scattering grain for a small flock of chickens.

Jim stepped quickly behind a large oak tree and pulled David after him. Without a word, the boys watched from behind the tree until the woman had scattered the last of her grain and disappeared into the house. As she closed the back door behind her, David caught a glimpse of a neat kitchen. He sighed longingly.

"I wonder if she'd sell us some food," he said softly. "I'm hungry enough to eat a horse."

"Me too," Jim whispered. "I don't dare ask her, though, Dave. She'd know for sure that I was running away."

"I'll ask her," David said, although for some reason he rather disliked the idea. "You wait here and I'll be back as soon as I can."

Jim nodded. "Better go up to the house from the road instead of across the yard," he advised. "You don't want her to know you came out of the woods, you know."

"Good idea," David agreed. And he started off through the trees that skirted the clearing.

Taking care to keep well hidden behind the big oak, Jim unbundled the black cape, wrapped himself up in it, and sat down at the foot of the tree to wait for David. How long he sat there, he never knew. But night had fallen and the stars were out when he heard the whistle which he and David had agreed earlier to use as a signal. He whistled softly in reply and stood up. An instant later David grabbed him by the arm. The younger boy was jubilant.

"Here," he exclaimed softly, thrusting a package into Jim's hand. "Bread, cheese, cold beefsteak, and a big piece of pie. Eat it all, Jim. Miss Peck made me eat some supper there in the kitchen, and then sold me this to eat tomorrow."

"Did she ask you any questions?" Jim inquired, breaking open the package eagerly.

"Some," David replied. "But I managed it so I didn't have to answer most of them. All I told her was that I had been to see my aunt and uncle, and was traveling home and had lost my way."

"That's good," Jim said, his mouth full of bread and cheese. "Was she there all alone?"

"Yes," answered David. "She has a father, and a brother named Bill, but they're both away. They rode off this morning to a big meeting at Fullerton about that man Douglas that everyone around here wants for President."

"Fullerton!" Jim repeated, looking up sharply.

"It's all right," David assured him quickly. "Miss Peck says they're going to stay there all night and won't be back till tomorrow noon. She told me I could sleep in the barn, too. I figured maybe we could both rest there and then start off again while it's still dark."

"Let's," said Jim, with a shiver. "I can eat there just as well as here, and I'm near froze to death. Just wait till I get my bonnet and dress."

Handing the package of food to David, he felt around on the ground until he found the dress and bonnet. Then, holding his cape around his shoulders, he followed David silently across the clearing and through the barn door.

The boys groped their way to the ladder, which David had located before he returned to Jim, and climbed to the hayloft. In a short time every crumb of Jim's supper had disappeared. And after agreeing that they would rest only half the night, and leave the barn long before daylight, both boys snuggled down deep in the hay. Worn out with the exciting events of the morning and their long journey through the woods, both of them were soon fast asleep.

David was the first to be awakened, several hours later, by a noise below them. Opening his eyes, he stared into the dark, not quite sure for a moment where he was. Then he remembered, and his heart leaped to his throat.

Two men were talking in the barn beneath him, and he realized with alarm that Miss Peck's father and her brother Bill had returned sooner than she had expected them. They were conversing together as they put their horses up for the night. Lying in the hay, tense with fright and terrified that Jim might awaken and speak, David strained his ears to hear what the men were saying.

"Too bad that speaker fellow didn't get there to hold the meeting tonight," remarked one man in a deep voice. "If us Democrats don't pull together better than we're doing now, that long-faced old Abe Lincoln will get himself elected next Tuesday, sure as my name is Jeremiah Peck."

"And then there'll be a mess of trouble!" exclaimed a voice which David knew must belong to Bill. "The slaveowners just ain't going to let a northern man be President, Pa. That's what a man was telling me tonight. They're getting more roiled up every day, with the Underground helping so many slaves run off, and the North being so uppity about sending them back. I don't blame 'em, either. Move over there, Dobbin."

To the ears of the frightened boy listening in the loft came the sound of Dobbin's hoofs on the wooden floor. There was a moment's silence. One of the horses neighed softly. Then Mr. Peck remarked with a laugh, "That Johnson fellow got himself a pretty-looking black eye in that stagecoach fight this morning, didn't he?"

"He sure did," agreed Bill, emphatically. "I'd like to see the man who did it."

"I'd rather lay my hands on the runaway," his father declared. "We could get us one of those newfangled McCormick reapers and a good team of mules with the reward his owner will pay to get him back. Well, shut up the barn when you've finished, Bill. I'll go wake your sister and tell her we're home."

Footsteps creaked across the barn floor. Bill began to whistle "Dixie" under his breath. Jim stirred in the hay and made a little noise in his sleep. And David, who was wishing with all his heart that Bill would get out of the barn, so that he and Jim might sneak away, smothered a sneeze. Just at that moment Mr. Peck's voice came from the direction of the barn door. He sounded bewildered and a little disturbed.

"Hey, Bill, where in tarnation do you suppose this black bonnet came from?" he asked. "I found it on the ground, right here by the barn door. It ain't your sister's, is it?"

"No, it don't look like Eliza's. It looks more like the bonnet Widow Sparks wears to church on Sunday," Bill answered slowly. Then, in a more excited tone, he added, "Say, Pa, those fellows who escaped from the stage this morning — folks said one of them was dressed like a widow-lady."

"Do you suppose —" Mr. Peck began. But Bill interrupted him.

"By gun!" he exclaimed. "I reckon it wasn't rats that I heard up in the hayloft a minute ago, after all. Hand me my old shotgun over there in the corner, Pa. And hold one of the lanterns for me. I'm going up to find out."

chapter 13

A Night of Suspense

M R. PECK held his lantern high and peered down at the two frightened figures which stood before him, with hands upraised.

"Lord save us, Bill, they're nothing but boys!" he exclaimed. "To hear Johnson talk you'd think they were a couple of big fellows like us."

"Boys or not, one of them is worth a good-sized reward," Bill said exultantly, lowering his shotgun.

He looked at Jim and David. "All right, you young rascals," he went on. "You can put your hands down. Now, leave those black clothes just where they're lying, get down the ladder, and follow my Pa into the house. I'll be close behind you every step of the way. And if one of you starts a ruckus or tries to run for it,

I'll fill the other one full of buckshot. Understand?"

Jim's brown eyes were terror-stricken. He swallowed hard and nodded his head miserably.

Trying to keep his voice steady, David stared at the huge, redheaded man who towered over him, and said, "Yes sir."

Thoroughly scared, and realizing that any attempt at escape would be useless at the moment, both boys reluctantly did as they were told. When they had followed Mr. Jeremiah Peck's tall, stooped figure down the ladder, across the yard, and into the neatly furnished kitchen, Bill gruffly commanded them to sit down on the floor, side by side, with their backs against the wall. Mr. Peck warned them not to move, and set his lantern down on the table.

"Eliza!" he shouted at the top of his lungs. "Eliza, wake up and come here."

"All right," called a sleepy voice from a room above. "I'm awake. I'm coming."

A bed creaked overhead. Footsteps padded down the hall stairs. And Eliza Peck, with a gray flannel robe over her high-necked bedgown, her nightcap slightly askew, and a candle in her hand, appeared in the doorway. At the sight of David, sitting on the floor beside Jim, she gave a little start of recognition. But she did not speak to him, and she stared at Jim curiously.

"Land sakes!" she exclaimed, looking at her father. "What's wrong, Pa? What's going on here?"

Mr. Peck ran a bony hand through his shaggy gray hair. "Just a couple of young ruffians we caught in the barn," he said. And, keeping an eye on the captives, he and Bill together told Miss Eliza Peck why they had come home unexpectedly and how they had discovered David and Jim in the hayloft.

During this conversation Bill had placed a straight-backed chair in front of the two forlorn-looking boys and had seated himself in it, resting his shotgun across his knees. Now, rubbing his big hands together, he looked gloatingly at Jim.

"Well," he said triumphantly, "seems like I've got the price of a new McCormick reaper, and maybe a pair of good mules, sitting right in front of me. Who's your owner, young fellow?"

Jim started to speak, glanced unhappily at David, and shook his curly black head.

"Not going to talk, eh?" remarked Mr. Peck, leaning on the back of Bill's chair. "Well, it don't matter, Bill. We can find out real easy, seeing as we know they got on the stage at Greenfield."

"But who helped them get started? That's what I want to know!" Bill exclaimed, glancing over his shoulder at his father. "If we can worm that out of them, we'll know who's running that blasted Underground in these parts. I aim to own some slaves myself, soon as I can make a pile of money and can take life easy, and I don't want any — " He swung around suddenly and glared at David. "Want to go to jail for stealing a slave?" he asked, abruptly.

David blinked his eyes. "No sir," he replied soberly.

"Well, you don't have to," Bill said in a more kindly

tone. "You can walk right out of this house, free, if you'll tell us just three things. Who owns your friend? Where did he get the widow's clothing he was running off in? And where were you planning to go for help when you reached Fullerton? Come on, boy. Three answers, and you can go free."

For an instant David did not reply. Then, drawing a deep breath, he answered bravely, "I'd — I'd never tell you what you want to know, if I went to jail for the rest of my life."

Bill's face turned crimson above his stubby red beard. "Is that so?" he exclaimed angrily. "You'll change your fine-sounding tune tomorrow, you young pup, when I fetch the sheriff. He'll make you talk, if he has to beat it out of you and lock you up, too."

He rubbed his nose. Then he leaned his face closer to David. "Are you sure you wouldn't want to change your mind and tell me what I want to know?" he asked in a wheedling voice.

"No sir," David replied stoutly, hoping that he didn't look or sound as frightened as he felt.

Bill scowled. Handing the gun to Mr. Peck, he stood up, grabbed Jim by the shoulder, dragged him to a standing position, and began to search his trousers pockets.

"These scoundrels may be carrying knives, and I ain't taking any chances," he explained to his father and sister, as he pulled out an old red bandanna in which Jim had tied his money, a rabbit's foot which the colored boy carried for luck, and some bits of string.

Tossing them to the kitchen table, he added, "We'll just turn these things over to the sheriff in the morning and let him do what he wants with them. All right you, sit down."

He gave Jim a little push and ordered David to stand up. Slowly the boy rose to his feet. Shutting his lips tightly together, he allowed Bill to take his purse, his pocketknife, his compass, his handkerchief, and several odds and ends, without a protest. But when Bill pulled the small gray dictionary from the back pocket of his trousers and put it on the table, the boy reached for it hastily. Just as hastily Bill gave David's arm a sharp crack with his big hand.

"Let that alone," he commanded.

"But it's not mine," David blurted out, rubbing his arm. "You can keep everything else, but the book's not mine. Please give it back to me."

For the first time since he and Jim had been discovered in the barn, tears rushed to David's eyes. He wiped them away hastily.

Bill laughed. "Oh, all right, baby," he said. "We ain't thieves, after all. I just want to make sure that you two ain't carrying anything that will help you get away from here." He thrust the book into David's hands. "Now, get back there next to your friend again," he ordered, as he took his gun from his father. David sat down.

By this time Miss Peck had ventured farther into the kitchen. Still holding her candle, she looked pityingly at Jim, who was trembling so much, either with a cold or with fright, that his teeth were chattering. Then she let her eyes rest for a long minute on David's face.

The boy returned her gaze unhappily, wondering why she was pretending she had never seen him before, and why she had not told her father and brother about giving him food. As she turned her eyes away from his, he thought hopefully for an instant that she had smiled at him. But the candle was flickering so that he could not be sure, and his hope died away when she spoke to her brother.

"They're a mean-looking pair of young'uns," she declared, "especially the white boy. Where are you going to put 'em for the rest of the night?"

Bill stroked the barrel of his shotgun thoughtfully. "Somewhere where they can't do any mischief," he replied. "I reckon the attic is the best place. There's a good bolt on the door, and nothing up there they can harm. How about it, Pa?"

"It sounds all right to me," Mr. Peck replied, holding his hands close to the big iron stove to warm them. "We don't want 'em to freeze, though. If that colored boy gets sick, he won't be no good to anybody. Fetch 'em each a blanket, Eliza. I'm going out to lock up the barn."

Eliza Peck nodded and went out of the kitchen by one door, while her father left by the other. Like a trapped animal, David glanced quickly around the room, thinking wildly that he and Jim could overpower Bill, now that they were alone with him, and find some means of escape. But, as if Bill read what was in the boy's mind, he patted his gun lovingly and made a playful clicking noise with his tongue.

David glared at him defiantly, but he sank back against the wall. Bill grinned, scratched his head, and yawned loudly. For several moments no one moved, and there were no sounds in the kitchen except the chattering of Jim's teeth, the ticking of the clock on a shelf in the corner, and the crackling of wood in the big stove. Then Miss Peck appeared in the doorway.

"I can't get the lid up on the chest those old blankets are stored in, Bill," she complained. "You must have jammed it shut some way when you mended it the other day. Give me your gun, and I'll watch these young varmints while you open it."

Mumbling something under his breath about useless women, Bill handed his gun to his sister and lumbered out of the room. Immediately Jim grabbed David by the arm and started to his feet.

"Now, you set right still there," Miss Peck commanded loudly, pointing the shotgun waveringly at Jim. "I can shoot as good as Bill can any day." Then she leaned forward. "Don't you see it won't do you no good?" she whispered earnestly. "One way you'll run into Pa, and the other way you'll run into Bill. They're real hard men when it comes to anything that means money, and you're no match for either of them."

"Let us go, ma'am," Jim pleaded, with something that sounded suspiciously like a sob in his voice. "Please let us go. Together, we —"

Miss Peck shook her head warningly. "You'd never make it," she whispered. "Do just like they tell you. I don't dare try to help you now, but later —"

She straightened up suddenly as heavy footsteps sounded in the front hall, and the back door creaked. When her father and Bill came into the kitchen at almost the same second, she was guarding the boys as though her very life depended on keeping them just where they were.

Bill took the gun from her and dumped two blankets in her lap. "Nothing wrong with that chest," he grumbled. "Bring the blankets and give us a light up the stairs."

Then he turned to the boys and motioned with his head toward the door. "On your feet," he commanded, "and follow my sister. It's after midnight and high time we got you two young lawbreakers locked up safe and sound, so's we can get some sleep around here."

David and Jim obediently stumbled to their feet. Miss Peck's half-spoken promise of help had given them each fresh courage. Yet, despite that promise, David looked about sharply as he followed the woman's flickering candle through the hall and up the stairs. Quickly he noted how the front door was fastened and where the bedrooms were placed. If there should be any chance for escape in the night, he wanted to be familiar enough with the house so that he wouldn't go blundering through the wrong door.

At the top of the stairs, Bill shoved both boys into the big, dark, musty-smelling attic. Taking the blankets from his sister, he thrust them into David's arms. Then he slammed the door and bolted it.

Crouching close together in the dark, David and Jim heard him clump down the stairs, and yell good night to his father. Next they heard Miss Peck's low voice going on and on, as though she were praying. And then the house was quiet.

For several minutes longer, Jim and David remained motionless and silent. Pale moonlight was filtering through a small, dusty window, and as the boys' eyes became accustomed to the half-darkness they saw that the big, slanting-roofed attic contained nothing whatever but three round-topped trunks. Closely followed by Jim, David groped his way around the trunks to the little window. He opened it cautiously and stuck his head out.

"It's a terrible drop to the ground," he whispered despairingly as he pulled his head in again.

"Reckon that mean old Bill knew that when he put us up here," Jim said softly. "Wish't we had a rope we could swing down on. Maybe there's something in them trunks we can use for rope. Like — like blankets, maybe."

"Blankets!" exclaimed David. "I dropped two blankets over there by the door when we —"

But Jim was already examining the blankets which had been given them by Miss Peck. "Just like I thought," he said mournfully. "They're so old and worn out that they wouldn't even hold the weight of a kitten."

"Let's try them, anyway," muttered David excitedly. "Take the other end of this one, Jim, and pull with all your might."

"Don't think it'll hold, but I'll try," whispered Jim. He seized one end of the blanket and pulled hard. It tore suddenly, and the boy went back, heels over head, on the floor with a thud that David thought could be heard half a mile away.

"Hurt?" he asked, bending over his friend.

"Ain't hurt, but plenty scared," replied Jim under his breath. "That noise will bring them all up here arunning. You just see if it don't."

The boys listened almost breathlessly for the pounding of angry feet on the stairs. But the only noise they heard was a muffled sound which could have been a man's hard laugh or the call of a wild animal in the woods.

"Well, we won't try that again," David said at last, with a sigh of relief.

"Reckon it's safe now to see what's in them trunks?" Jim whispered.

"Yes," murmured David, helping the other boy to his feet. He and Jim stole across the attic floor on tiptoe. Together they tugged at the lid of each round-topped trunk, but with no success. All three were securely locked.

David looked around the attic and shook his head mournfully. "There isn't any way we can get out of this dratted place!" he exclaimed under his breath. "Not any way at all, unless Miss Peck —"

"Miss Peck!" Jim interrupted shortly. "She's scared to death of her men folks. Chances are she'll never come near us. I don't know what we're going to do, Davy, but there ain't nobody going to take me back to Mr. Cooper, nor you to jail, neither."

Crossing to the window, he looked out again. "Nope," he said, shutting it softly, "there ain't no use. We'd just break our legs and be worse off than we are now." He shivered. "Lawsy, it's cold," he added, "and we've only got one blanket left now."

David reached for the blanket. "You take it," he said, wrapping it around Jim's shoulders. "You haven't any coat, and my jacket keeps me warm enough."

Pulling the blanket gratefully about him, Jim squatted down on the floor. David sat down beside him, hunched up his knees, and rested his head wearily on his folded arms, trying, rather hopelessly, to figure out what to do next. For a long time neither he nor Jim spoke. Each was busy with his own thoughts, and they were not pleasant ones.

In spite of his talk about not going back to Mr. Cooper, Jim was seeing dismal pictures in his mind, of himself being carried back to Greenfield, being cruelly beaten because he had run away, and being taken in handcuffs far, far south to Texas. David was wondering gloomily how he could get word to his grandfather after he had been arrested, whether his mother and Nancy would cry when they heard the news, and what would happen to him in jail.

Outside an owl hooted again and again in a nearby

tree, and the wind made a mournful sighing sound. In a room below, a man snored steadily. Unable to keep his eyes open, David drowsed, half asleep and half awake. He had almost forgotten where he was when suddenly Jim gave a little exclamation of alarm and grabbed his arm.

"Ghosts!" Jim moaned softly, pointing a trembling finger. "Ghosts! Look!"

David looked quickly. And such a feeling of relief swept over him at the sight of a tall, gray figure coming through the half-open attic door that he could hardly restrain a shout of joy.

"It's Miss Peck," he whispered, getting carefully and quietly to his feet.

Moving like the ghost Jim had thought she was, Miss Peck closed the door softly behind her and approached the boys on tiptoe. She thrust a heavy jacket into Jim's arms.

"Take it," she said, speaking so low that the boys could hardly hear her. "It's an old one of Bill's. Serves him right to lose it, too."

"Can we go now?" David whispered eagerly.

Miss Peck nodded. "I couldn't get your money or your things for you, though," she said. "Bill took them all to bed with him. But here's food — enough to last you a whole day if you're careful — and some lucifer matches in case you get where you can light a fire."

"Thank you," David whispered, taking the package of food in one hand and pocketing the matches with the other. "What's the best way to head when we go?"

Instead of replying, Miss Peck caught Jim by the shoulder just as the boy was turning up the sleeves of Bill's heavy jacket.

"Reckon you know why I'm letting you go, don't you?" she asked, peering earnestly in the half-darkness at his brown face.

" 'Cause you're a kind lady," Jim murmured impatiently, looking longingly at the door.

Miss Peck gave him a little shake. "I'm letting you go because the Bible says all men are brothers. And good folks don't let their brothers get bought and sold like animals, if they can help it. The Lord wouldn't like it."

"No ma'am. He wouldn't," Jim said, wishing with all his heart that the woman would stop talking and send them on their way.

"Now, listen sharp," Miss Peck went on. "Creep down the stairs as quiet as you can. You'll find the front door open. When you get to the road, turn right and run like you've never run before."

"We'll run, all right," David promised softly. "Can we go now?"

"Yes," whispered Miss Peck. "Get as far away as you can before morning, though. Bill will set out looking for you as soon as he finds you've gone."

She took her hand from Jim's shoulder. "Go on," she said. "I'll wait here till you're safe outside. Then I'll open the window and bolt this door and let that wicked Bill wonder tomorrow how you managed to get away."

Jim nodded gratefully and started to tiptoe toward the door. Just then David grabbed his arm.

"Wait!" he said softly. "We'd better take off our shoes."

Hastily the boys removed their heavy boots. Then, moving like shadows, they slipped out of the attic and felt their way down the steep stairs which led to the second floor. David was in the lead. His heart beat loudly as he crept past the bedroom doors, and it seemed to him that Jim's heavy breathing close behind him could be heard all over the house.

Halfway down the hall, he stepped on a squeaky board. Both boys froze to stillness, sure that the noise had awakened either Bill or Mr. Peck. But the steady snoring in one bedroom continued, and no sound came from behind the closed door of the other. Stealthily the boys tiptoed down the second flight of stairs, across the hall, and through the open door. Without a word, they broke into a run.

They did not stop until they had gone a good distance down the road. Then, squatting on the ground, they put on their shoes. Never had the stars looked as bright to David as they did at that moment. Never had the air smelled so sweet.

"Hey, Jim!" he exclaimed joyously, tugging at a shoelace, "Jim, we're free!"

Jim shook his head. "Not till we get across that big old river and into Illinois, we ain't," he said. "An' I won't feel like I'm honest-to-goodness free till I get clear to Canada. Come on, hurry up." And, pulling David to his feet, he started off again at a run.

chapter *14*

A Lucky Tumble

I<small>T WAS</small> after seven o'clock in the evening, but the streets in the center of Chicago were filled with people, cheering, singing, and shouting with joy. Huge bonfires were thrusting great tongues of flame into the cool night air. Roman candles spangled the dark with showers of sparks and bright-colored balls. Fountains of light spurted high, fizzed, and died down again. Rockets streaked across the black sky, breaking overhead into splashes of glittering rain and golden stars.

Women exclaimed softly over the beautiful fireworks and children squealed with delight. Suddenly in the distance there was a burst of music.

"Hurrah!" shouted someone in the crowd. "Here come the Wide-Awakes!"

And there they came! Thousands of them, marching down the street in a zigzag fashion, so that their blazing torches looked like a huge, writhing dragon of light.

Robbie Morgan, who was hanging onto his grandfather's hand tightly, sighed with happiness.

"Jingoes!" he shouted to Peter, who stood beside him, hanging onto Nancy. "I'm glad Mr. Lincoln was elected. Aren't you?"

Peter nodded, far too excited to speak, but not too excited to open his mouth wide and join in the singing when the band began to play:

> Old Abe Lincoln came out of the wilderness
> Out of the wilderness, out of the wilderness,
> Old Abe Lincoln came out of the wilderness,
> Down in Illinois.

But all the people in the crowd were not singing. Many were worried, even though they rejoiced that Abraham Lincoln was to be the next President of the United States.

"What with all this talk from South Carolina about seceding, I don't know that there'll be a United States by the time old Abe gets to Washington," a man standing next to Grandfather remarked, as the Wide-Awakes swung by.

"Nonsense!" snorted Grandfather. "There'll always be a United States, even if we have to fight a war to keep it united. We can't just let this country break up into pieces every time states disagree with each other. Look out there, Peter. You'll get stepped on by that officer's horse."

He reached out, grabbed Peter by the shoulder, and pulled him back on the sidewalk. Then, looking down at Mrs. Morgan, who stood just behind Nancy, he said, "I think we'd better start home, don't you? The boys have seen about all there is to see."

Mrs. Morgan and Nancy both nodded, and despite loud protests from Peter and Robbie, all five began to work their way through the crowd, toward State Street.

"Oh, I do wish Davy were here," Nancy exclaimed, as soon as they had left the crowd behind them and were able to walk and talk together. "He won't like missing all this excitement a bit. When do you think he'll come home, Grandfather?"

"Don't know, and I wish you'd stop asking me," Grandfather replied, rather crossly.

Although the old gentleman would not admit it to anyone, he had been troubled about David ever since the boy's letter had arrived from St. Louis. And he sounded quite provoked as he added, "It all depends, I suppose, on what luck he has in finding Jim."

Mother clutched at her bonnet as a stiff wind blew it back from her face. "We should never have let him go," she said in a worried tone. "I knew it all the time. That friend he wrote about — how do we know what kind of person he is? Maybe he'll rob him or —"

"Nonsense!" Grandfather broke in testily. "You act like a hen with one chicken, Susan. Stop fretting about the boy. He's got a good head on his shoulders. David's all right."

And at that particular moment David *was* all right. Four nights and days had passed since he and Jim had escaped from the Pecks' farm. Four nights and days of tramping through the woods, stealing at night along winding country roads, sleeping under thickets and bushes whenever they could go no farther, and eating whatever they could lay their hands on.

By managing carefully, they had made the food Miss Peck had given them last for two days. In the woods they had found nuts and wild grapes, and Jim had caught a rabbit, which he roasted over a small campfire. Both boys were afraid, however, that the smoke from their fire might be seen and lead to their discovery. So they had only half cooked the animal, and it had proved so tough that they could eat little of it. It had been enough, however, to give them strength to keep going.

Now, in spite of the fact that they were ravenously hungry and so tired that David said he felt as if his legs didn't belong to him at all, they were happy. For, after skirting a little village, they had come suddenly to the edge of a wooded bluff. Below them, reflecting a pale yellow moon, lay a broad, smooth ribbon of water.

"It's that old Mississippi, sure enough," Jim said joyfully. "And look, Davy! There, way over on the other side — that's Illinois! That's freedom!"

David nodded. "That's right!" he said excitedly.

"All we have to do now is to get there," Jim went on. "Come on, Dave."

Pushing through the bushes, Jim started to climb carefully down the bluff. It was steep and rocky and slippery. But he reached the bottom in safety, and turned to look out over the water.

"Lawsy!" he said in an awed voice, "it's an awful wide river, Dave. How do you think we'll ever get across?"

His only answer was a cry of alarm. Swinging around on his heel, he saw that David had missed his footing halfway down the bluff. Rolling over and over in a shower of rocks, the boy came tumbling to the ground, landed in a heap at Jim's feet, and lay still.

Jim leaned over him anxiously. "Are you all right, Dave?" he asked. Receiving no reply, he dropped to his knees. "Davy, speak to me," he begged, his voice hoarse with terror. "Open your eyes, Dave. Are you all right?"

David moaned softly, but he neither spoke nor raised his eyelids. Panic-stricken, Jim rushed to the river, filled his hands with water, and splashed it over the boy's face. Then, dropping to his knees again, he rubbed David's hands between his own, felt him all over to see if any bones were broken, and smoothed his forehead, talking to him all the while. But David never stirred.

"I got to get him to someone who can help him," Jim thought desperately. "And then they'll catch us, and that'll be the end of everything. But he can't lie

here like this. He'll die, maybe. I got to get someone
who can help him."

Hastily removing his jacket, he laid it over David's
still form. Then he looked about, wondering whether
it would be better to scramble up the steep bluff and
run to the village for help, or whether he could reach
the little town more quickly by following the river
shore.

"Reckon the river way is fastest," he said half aloud.
And with a last look at David, he started to run along
the rock-strewn riverbank. It jutted out into the water
slightly. Jim rounded the little bend. Suddenly his
heart leaped to his throat. There before him, not fifty
yards away, lay something both he and David had
dreamed about — something they had talked of longingly as they had made their way over weary miles
toward the river. A boat! A boat to carry them across
the Mississippi! If there should be oars in it, then
nothing could keep him from getting himself and
David safely to Illinois and freedom!

With a little cry of joy, Jim ran toward the rowboat
and laid his hand on the bow. At the same moment, a
tall, thin man stepped out from behind a nearby tree,
a hand grasped Jim's shoulder firmly, and a low, half-
joking voice said, "So you're one of the young imps
who've been stealing my boat at night to go fishing,
eh Dick? I thought if I hung around long enough I'd
catch one of you."

"No sir," said Jim, half sobbing now, and too tired
and discouraged to try to get away. "I didn't never

steal your boat, honest. I was just agoin' to borrow it. My friend —"

Gently the man swung Jim around so that he could see his face. Then he whistled softly under his breath. "Say!" he drawled, "I thought you were Mammy Sarah's boy, Dick. Who are you, youngster? You aren't a runaway, are you?"

Jim choked back a sob, but did not answer. The man gave him a little shake. "Speak up, boy, you don't need to be afraid of me," he said. "If you're aiming for the Illinois shore, I'll —" He looked around quickly. "Is anyone following you?" he asked.

Jim shook his head. "No sir," he said, "I —"

But the man did not give him time to finish. "Then come along with me," he commanded. "Hurry! My wife will fix you up with hot food and a coat of some kind. And I'll take you safe —"

"I can't do it, mister," Jim interrupted. "There's Davy. He's lying on the ground back there, and he's hurt, and —"

"So there are *two* of you!" the man exclaimed. "Well, if you're sure there's no one on your trail, take me to your friend quickly, and we'll find out what's wrong with him."

Still a little bewildered by this unexpected turn of events, Jim led the way, as fast as he could, to the place where he had left David. The other boy was sitting up by this time, with both hands clasped to his head.

"Hello," he murmured in a queer slow voice when Jim reached him. "I feel like I —"

"Don't talk, Dave," Jim said, slipping an arm around David's shoulders. "Here's someone to help you. Can you stand up?"

"I'll — I'll try," David answered shakily. He made a feeble attempt to get to his feet, then fell back on the ground again.

Just then the stranger caught sight of David's face. "On my soul, he's white!" he exclaimed softly. "Is he running off with you?"

"No," said Jim. "Not exactly. We're — we're friends." Then, catching the man's arm, he begged, "Don't let anybody send him to jail for helping me, mister. I'll go back to Master Cooper again, if I have to, but don't let anybody hurt Davy."

"I'm not going to let anybody hurt either of you if I can help it," the man declared, stooping down and gathering David's limp form in his arms. "Make haste there, boy. Pick up your jacket and come along. It's not far."

With Jim stumbling along beside him and with David in his arms, the man strode along the river shore until they had passed the beached rowboat. Then they climbed up a steep path which led to a comfortable-looking brick house. When he reached the front door of the house, he struck at it gently with his foot.

"Mary," he called softly. "Mary, I've brought visitors. Let us in quickly."

It seemed to Jim, who was worried about David and wondering unhappily what was going to happen next, that the woman called Mary would never open the door. But of course she did — and almost immediately. Strangely enough, she did not seem in the least surprised when she spied Jim standing on the threshold. But she cried out softly when she caught sight of her husband's limp burden.

"Why, Seth Howland!" she exclaimed, shutting the door hastily. "Where did that white boy come from? Is he badly hurt? No, don't stop to tell me now. Bring him upstairs, and we'll get him right to bed."

She picked up a lamp from the hall table. Then she glanced rapidly from Jim to her husband. "Did anyone see you come in?" she asked.

"No," replied Mr. Howland. "Are all the window curtains pulled shut?"

"Of course," answered his wife, and started up the stairs. Carrying David carefully, Mr. Howland followed her, with Jim close at his heels.

Half an hour later, David was tucked in bed with a warm brick at his feet and a cool, wet bandage laid over the huge bump which was rising on his bruised and aching head. And Jim, who had explained to Mr. Howland all about himself and David, was sitting at the kitchen table, devouring ham, eggs, fried potatoes, great slices of buttered bread, and fresh doughnuts. As he ate, washing the food down with great gulps of hot coffee, he looked warily about the kitchen, not able yet to believe that he was safe and among friends.

"Maybe they're just goin' to hold me here till they can fetch a sheriff, and then send me back to Master

Cooper's," he thought uneasily. "If it weren't for Davy lying up there, I'd get out of here right now."

Perhaps Mrs. Howland, who was standing at the stove warming some milk for David, guessed at that moment what was in the boy's mind, for she caught his eye and smiled at him.

"Come here, Jim," she said, pushing the pan of milk to the back of the stove. "I want to show you something."

Hastily swallowing a mouthful of bread, Jim got to his feet and followed her into the hall.

"Put your hand there," Mrs. Howland told him, pointing to what looked like a knothole in the paneling under the stairs. "That's right. Now, push."

Jim obeyed wonderingly. Then he exclaimed in surprise. Before his bewildered eyes a low, narrow door swung open, revealing a cubbyhole containing a small table with a candle on it, and a cot.

"It's a hideaway!" Jim cried softly.

"That's right," agreed Mrs. Howland. "Sometimes, when the weather is very bad, we keep runaways here two or three days before Mr. Howland can get them safely across the river."

She pulled the door shut. "Well, now you know about the little room," she went on. "If anyone comes to the house while you are waiting for David's head to heal, don't waste a minute. Hide in there, and keep as still as you can until we tell you it's safe to come out."

"Yes ma'am," Jim said. Tears of relief had flooded his eyes, and he wiped them away quickly on the back of his hand. "Now I know for sure that we are back on the tracks of that old Underground Railroad," he added with a smile. "Can I go tell Davy?"

Mrs. Howland nodded, and Jim went upstairs to tell David the good news. But the injured boy was so drowsy that he hardly seemed to hear him at all.

Indeed, nearly a week passed before David was strong enough so that the boys could start north again. During the early part of that week Mr. Howland wrote a short letter to Grandfather Morgan, telling him about David's accident, and assuring him that the boys were safe and would soon start home. But when he wanted to put a line in the letter, asking Mr. Morgan to send money for the boys' railway fare from Carlinville — the nearest railway station — David begged him not to do it.

"Grandpa gave me all the money he could spare when I started out," David said. "Jim and I can work our way home somehow, once we get into Illinois. Can't we, Jim?"

Jim grinned. "I reckon with me to look after you, and you to look after me, we can do 'most anything," he said. "Just you lie quiet now, and get well."

For Jim, the days of waiting seemed endless. He was restless and uneasy. Of course he could not leave the house, and several times when neighbors came to call he had to spend an hour or more in the tiny, airless room under the stairs.

The only excitement during the whole time occurred one dark, rainy night. Then, in answer to a mysterious tapping on the kitchen window, Mrs. Howland opened the door to let in two terrified colored women and a young colored boy. All three had run away from a place in southern Missouri, and had been sent to Mr. Howland by another conductor on the Underground Railroad.

They were frightened, cold, wet, and tired. But they were so anxious to get farther north that they begged to be taken across the river at once, and did not even wait to eat the meal which Mrs. Howland had started to prepare for them.

Jim watched them with envy when they set out for the rowboat in which Mr. Howland was going to take them across the Mississippi. In spite of the Howlands' kindness, the boy longed to be on his way. But when Mrs. Howland suggested that he cross the river and head north with the fugitives, he shook his head.

"No'm. I'll just wait for Davy, if you don't mind my staying here," he said.

Fortunately he did not have to wait much longer, for the very next day David was able to get up. And two days later Mrs. Howland said he was well enough to start the journey home. That night, after a big supper, Mr. Howland gave the boys careful directions for finding a certain house on the other side of the river, where they would be given shelter for the night. Mrs. Howland filled their pockets with food and made David promise to write to her as soon as he reached Chicago. And then they set out with Mr. Howland in the rowboat.

Never, as long as they lived, did either David or Jim forget the long, slow trip across the Mississippi River, with Jim crouched in the bottom of the boat, ready to hide himself under a dark blanket if any other boat should approach them. Never did they forget the wonderful feeling of relief which swept over them when they felt the Illinois shore beneath their feet. Never did they forget the many people who helped them, or the exciting things that happened to them, as they made their way north to Chicago in the days that followed.

Even though Jim was in a free state and had his freedom paper with him, Mr. Howland had warned him that he had better follow the Underground until he was many miles from Missouri. So, for several days, Jim and David went just where they were sent by the brave men and women who were using their homes as stations on the railroad to freedom.

They spent one night in a hunter's shack on the edge of a prairie. And they were hidden all the next day in a cave nearby, while slave catchers from St. Louis searched for a runaway who had been traced to that neighborhood. They rode through a goodsized town in broad daylight, with a gray-clad Quaker who hid Jim away under the seat of his buggy. And once, when slave catchers were hot on the trail of two fugitives from Kentucky, David himself was put in charge of a farmer's wagon, and drove it from one station to the next, with Jim and the runaways hidden among some sacks of grain.

What with one thing and another, nearly ten days passed before the two weary, dirty, disheveled boys reached Chicago. It was evening when they said "Thank you" and "Good-by" to a friendly doctor who had given them a lift on the last lap of their journey. Tired as he was, David broke into a run as he turned into State Street and neared home.

"Come on, Jim," he cried. "Jingoes, I'll be glad to see Ma and the others."

"Me, too," Jim agreed with a grin.

A moment later both boys were pounding on the kitchen door.

chapter 15

The End of the Line

I T WAS NANCY who opened the door. For an instant she stared at the two grinning young tramps on the doorstep as though she couldn't believe her eyes. Then she shouted joyfully, "Mother! Grandpa! It's Davy and Jim! It's Davy and Jim!"

With a little cry of joy, Mrs. Morgan dropped the shirt she was mending and flew to the door. Grandfather dropped his book to the floor and hurried after her. Robbie and Peter fell over each other in their efforts to reach David first. And even Inky left her warm spot under the stove, arched her back, and came out to meow a welcome.

At first, of course, everyone talked and asked questions at once. Nancy pulled her brother into the house and hung onto his arm as if she'd never let go again. Robbie and Peter grabbed his other arm. Mrs. Morgan

planted a hasty kiss on David's forehead and reached
out a hand to Jim, laughing and crying at the same
time. And Grandfather caught David to him in a
great hug, patted Jim on the shoulder, and said over
and over, beaming proudly all the while, "I knew
they'd make it. I knew they'd get back safely."

At last the excitement died down. Nancy brought
a kettle of warm water from the stove so that the
boys could wash away some of the dirt which had
accumulated since they had left the Howlands in
Missouri. Mother put fresh bread, butter, cold chicken,
ham, gingerbread, cheese, milk, and cookies on the
table. And then everyone sat down to listen while
David and Jim, between mouthfuls of supper, told
how they had met in Greenfield, what had happened
to each of them before they met, and how they had
finally reached home.

There was so much to tell, and everyone had so
many questions to ask and answer, that the talking
went on long after the boys had finished their supper
and the dishes were cleared away. Peter finally fell
asleep on Grandfather's knee. And Robbie, who was
determined not to miss anything, kept trying in every
way he could think of to keep himself awake. At last
he rubbed his eyes so hard that stars danced in front
of them, and that reminded him of something he
wanted to tell David.

"Davy," he said, pulling on his brother's sleeve to
attract his attention, "we saw fireworks and miles of
Wide-Awakes in a big parade for Mr. Lincoln."

"Did you, Robbie?" David asked, patting the little boy's hand. "I wish we'd seen it. But we knew he was elected all right, didn't we, Jim?"

Jim nodded. But before he had time to tell where they had learned of Lincoln's election, Grandfather spoke up.

"By the way, David," he said, "whatever happened to Mr. Lincoln's little dictionary? Was that lost along with the carpetbag?"

"No sir," David replied. Reaching into his back pocket, he pulled out the small gray book. "I took it out of the bag just before that man in the stagecoach yanked Jim's veil off," he explained. Then he went on to describe how he had tried to hide Jim's telltale foot from the prying eyes of Mr. Johnson.

Nancy watched him proudly all the time he was talking. "I'd never have been able to think of anything so clever," she declared.

David grinned, and his face flushed with pleasure. But all he said was, "Well, it didn't work, Nance. It was too late to do any good."

He held out the book to his grandfather. "I'm awful sorry I didn't get it to Mr. Lincoln in Springfield, the way you wanted me to," he apologized. "And it got a little dirty, I'm afraid, riding around in my pocket so long."

"It can be cleaned up, I think, and we'll mail it to Springfield," Grandfather said, shifting Peter on his knee so that the sleeping child could rest more comfortably. "Of course, I don't know that Mr. Lincoln would want it, now that he's going to move to Washington. But it's his, and I'd like to get it to him. Put it in my desk, please, lad."

Stepping over Inky, who lay purring near the stove, David carried the book to Grandfather's room and put it away. When he returned to the kitchen, Mother was talking to Jim about Mr. Cooper's farm in Greenfield. And then Jim asked the question which David had been dreading all the evening to hear:

"Do you think I could get to Canada soon, Mr. Morgan? Could you help me get aboard a boat like you helped Mark and Dora?"

Grandfather stroked his beard thoughtfully. "Yes, Jim," he said slowly, "I can even help you get to the town where Mark and Dora have settled, I think. But we'd like to have you stay on here with us, you know. Are you sure you want to go?"

Jim nodded soberly, glancing at David, and then looking away quickly as he realized for the first time how much he was going to miss his friend. "Yes, I want to go," he said. "This time I aim to ride that old secret railway to the very last station. It will be safe there, sure enough. There won't be no Snivelys, and —"

"But Jim —" David interrupted. Then he caught his lip between his teeth and shook his head sadly, as though he knew it would be useless to urge Jim not to go. Grandfather sighed, and a vague sense of unhappiness settled on the little group. Suddenly Mother caught sight of the unhappy expression in David's eyes.

Making up her mind quickly that the first evening the boys were back should not end gloomily, she stood up.

"Mercy on us!" she exclaimed, glancing at the clock. "It's been nearly four hours since these boys had supper, and they must be starving again after all their traveling.

"Robbie, set some plates and cups and saucers on the table. Nancy, you go into the shop and get that big white cake I made for Mrs. Brown — I'll bake her another early tomorrow. Poke up the fire, Davy, and Jim, you pump some water. I'll make a big pot of chocolate, and after Grandfather puts that sleepy Peter to bed the rest of us will have a homecoming celebration, even if it is nearly eleven o'clock."

So everyone jumped up and went to work. Grandfather carried Peter to bed, and before long the chocolate was ready and the cake was cut. The boys described details of their journey which they had not remembered earlier in the evening, and the subject of Jim's departure to Canada was not mentioned again.

The next morning, however, true to his promise, Grandfather went to find out about ships which were Canada-bound. When he returned to the house at noon, he reported that the *Michigan Belle*, which stopped at a port near the village where Mark and his wife had settled, was leaving two days later. The captain was willing to take Jim along.

"Captain Blake says that since you have your freedom paper, you can help out in the galley and work your passage that way," Grandfather told Jim. "The ship is not sailing till evening, but he wants you to be aboard by nine in the morning." Then, turning to Mrs. Morgan, the old gentleman added, "The boy will need warmer clothes than those he's wearing, Susan. Can we help him out?"

Mrs. Morgan nodded. And that evening after the shop was closed, Jim stood still while she turned up a pair of Grandfather's heavy trousers and measured his arm so that she could shorten the sleeves of the jacket Miss Peck had given him. The following evening the clothes were ready to wear. And early the next morning, right after the younger boys had gone to school, Jim and David set out together for the *Michigan Belle*.

It was a bleak November day, and the boys said little as they made their way toward the wharf at the foot of Clark Street, where the boat was moored. Jim was carrying an old bag of Grandfather's, in which Nancy had packed some of David's warm underwear, one of his flannel shirts, and some woolen socks. David, with both hands plunged deeply in his jacket pockets, plodded along beside him, thinking miserably that once Jim boarded the boat he probably never would see him again.

"Will you get someone to write a letter when you get to Canada, like Mark did, and tell us how you like it?" David asked, as they reached the wharf.

"I'll write it myself, soon as I can spell out enough words," Jim promised. "Well —" He stopped and set down his bag. "Here's the old boat. Reckon here's where we got to say 'good-by.'"

David nodded. For an instant the two boys looked at each other in silence. Then Jim said shyly, "I declare, Davy, I —"

At that very instant a tug close by whistled shrilly. Both boys jumped, and Jim grinned sheepishly. Then he began again.

"Listen, Dave, someday let's —"

David blinked his eyes. "Yes," he said. "Someday, we'll —" He swallowed hard. All at once he blurted out "'By, Jim. Good — good luck!" Swinging around on his heel suddenly, he ran down the street without once looking back.

"No use to stand there acting like a silly girl," he told himself angrily, rubbing his eyes on the sleeve of his jacket and slowing down to a walk as he reached the corner.

He was on Lake Street now, and he wandered aimlessly along the busy thoroughfare, wondering forlornly what Jim was doing, now that he was aboard the *Michigan Belle,* and what he himself should do with the long day which stretched ahead of him. Mother and Nancy would be working in the kitchen or the shop, and he would only be in their way if he went home. Grandfather would be busy writing his book and impatient of interruptions. Robbie, Peter, and most of the other boys in the neighborhood would be in school. There was no place in particular for David to go and nothing in particular for him to do. He was lonesome and unhappy.

"Well, there's the Tremont House. Guess I'll go find out if Mr. Adams is still working in the livery stable and tell him about Jim," he thought. Crossing the street, he went down the alley which led to the stable yard.

As usual at that time in the morning, this was a busy place, with carriages coming and going, stable boys harnessing and unharnessing horses, and coachmen standing about talking and waiting for orders.

David's face brightened when he saw Mr. Adams, just outside the stable door, hitching a fine pair of grays to a shiny closed carriage and whistling a Wide-Awake marching song as he worked. Stepping up behind him, the boy said, "Hello, Mr. Adams. Need any help?"

Mr. Adams looked around and smiled so broadly that his face crinkled up into scores of tiny crisscross lines.

"Mornin', young feller," he said in his high, cracked voice. "Ain't laid eyes on you for a long time. Nope, don't need any help on this job. Hop out of my way, there. I've got to see that everything on this outfit is first-class and shipshape." He tightened a harness strap and stepped back to examine the horses and carriage. "'Tain't often I get to hitch up a team for a man like him," he added, rubbing a speck of dirt from one of the brass lamps.

"What man are you talking about?" David asked, leaning down to scratch the ears of a black-spotted coach dog which was nosing his leg.

With a mischievous twinkle in his eyes, Mr. Adams replied, "Oh, just the man who's going to be President, that's all. Just Mr. Abraham Lincoln."

"Mr. Lincoln!" David repeated excitedly. "Is he here? Where is he? How long is he going to stay?"

"Don't know how long he's going to stay," Mr. Adams replied, ignoring the first two questions. "All I know is he wants a carriage ready in half an hour to carry him to the Wigwam, so's he can look over the place where he got nominated. And I aim to have it ready, too. Fetch me a currycomb, young feller. This horse's mane ain't right."

But Mr. Adams' request for a currycomb went unheeded, for David was already racing down the alley and heading for home as fast as his legs would carry him. He burst into the kitchen, passed Nancy without a word, and thrust open the door of Grandfather's room, not even stopping to knock.

"Give me Mr. Lincoln's dictionary, please, Grandpa," he panted. "He's — he's right here in Chicago at the — at the Tremont House. I can take it to him now, and —"

"Wait a minute," Grandfather said slowly, laying down his pen. "There's no need to act as if you were going to a fire."

"But — but don't you see?" David said, with an impatient grin. "I can hand the book right to him now. I can — jingoes, maybe I can even talk to him, Grandpa!"

"Not with your hair looking like that and those old

clothes on," Grandfather said. "Go and get yourself
fixed up, lad, while I clean up the book. Then you can
take it."

So David ran upstairs. A few moments later, dressed
in his best clothes, with his hair slicked down neatly
and the gray dictionary in his pocket, he was on his
way up State Street. Nancy was with him, for as soon
as she had learned where he was going and why, she
had begged to go along.

"Reckon the surest way to catch him now is to go
straight to the Wigwam," David said, grabbing her
elbow and turning into Monroe Street.

Nancy nodded, and the two hurried on without further words, past the new post office and customhouse,
up one street and down another, until they came in
sight of the Wigwam. Then David gave a sigh of relief.

"He's there," he said, breaking into a run. "That's
his carriage."

"What are you going to say to him?" Nancy asked,
hurrying to keep up with her brother.

"Don't know yet," David replied. "I won't know till
I get there."

But even after Nancy and David had reached the
Wigwam and stepped through an open door into the
vast, dusky hall, David was not quite sure how he
would approach Mr. Lincoln. To his great disappointment, Abraham Lincoln was not alone. Several men
and two women were grouped around the tall, stooped,
black-coated figure of the President-elect. And all were
listening while one of the men in the party pointed out

various things of interest in the building.

"That must be Mr. Lincoln's wife standing near him — that lady with the pretty bonnet trimmed with black," Nancy whispered as she and David shyly watched the group from the shadow of the balcony.

David nodded, but said nothing. He had no eyes for Mrs. Lincoln. His heart was pounding as he wondered if he dared step up and speak to the great man beside her, with so many people standing around watching and listening. At last, summoning up his courage, he touched Nancy's arm. "Come on, Nance," he said, and started across the hall.

The little group of sightseers was walking toward the long platform now, with Abraham Lincoln towering over them all. They were so busy, talking and laughing over some joke which Mr. Lincoln had just told, that they did not see the boy and girl approaching them, until Nancy suddenly tripped over a loose floor board and fell in a sprawling heap.

"God bless us!" exclaimed a jolly-looking gentleman, turning around quickly. "A lady in distress!" And stepping up to Nancy, he helped her to her feet before David could collect his wits.

"Did you hurt yourself?" he asked.

Nancy shook her head and straightened her bonnet, her face red with embarrassment.

"Then run along," the man said firmly. "This is no place for youngsters, and Mr. Lincoln doesn't want to be bothered with anyone today." Laying one hand on Nancy's arm and another on David's, he started to

walk with them to the door. But David held back.

"I've got to see Mr. Lincoln," he declared. "Please let go of me. I've got to see him."

"What about, boy?" asked a slow, kind voice just behind him. "What'd you want to see me for?"

Whirling around, David looked up and up into one of the kindest, saddest, most friendly faces he had ever laid eyes on. It was a face that made him feel good all over — a face that made him forget he had ever been afraid of anything. His heart stopped pounding, and he smiled a slow smile at the great man who was smiling down at him.

"What did you want to see me for?" Mr. Lincoln asked again, leaning down to brush some dust from Nancy's cape.

"This," David said. He fumbled in his pocket and pulled out the small gray book. "You left it in our shop one day when you came to buy some candy, and Nancy found it on the counter and — and it's yours."

"Why, so it is," Mr. Lincoln declared, taking the book in his big hand and flipping through the pages. "You know, I've often wondered where this little book went to. Many a time it's helped me out when I didn't know how to spell a word or wanted to find out the meaning of one."

"I'm sorry the book's a little dirty," Nancy said, suddenly feeling very much at home with this tall man. "You see, Davy carried it with him when he went —"

"Listen, Abe." The man who had helped Nancy up from the floor and who was still standing close by, put his hand on Lincoln's arm. "I'm afraid if you don't come now, we'll be late getting to — "

"All right, Ed," Mr. Lincoln replied. "I'm coming." Then, looking down at David again, he said, "Tell you what, son. I've got another dictionary at home. Why don't you just hand onto this and use it to help you with your lessons in school?"

"You mean I can keep it?" David asked, his eyes shining. Then his face fell. "Only — well, you see, I don't go to school."

Mr. Lincoln shook his head sympathetically. "That's too bad, my boy," he said. "Why not? Did your folks have to put you to work?"

"No sir," David replied, looking very ill at ease. "Not — not exactly. I — just don't like school."

"Hmm! That's a pity," Mr. Lincoln remarked soberly. "Our country's going to be in sore need of men who've had a good education. If you should decide you'd like to grow up to be one of them, maybe this book will help you the way it helped me. Here, take it, son."

David took the book and stared at it for a moment without a word. Ever since a certain day in April, eight months earlier, a guilty feeling that he had left a job half done had swept over him whenever anyone had mentioned school. Now, suddenly, that feeling was gone, leaving in its place a warm sense of comfort. He raised his eyes slowly to the wise, kind face above him.

"I reckon I've decided already, Mr. Lincoln," he said. "I'm going to need this book a lot. Thank you."

"Good!" exclaimed Abraham Lincoln, smiling broadly and holding out his hand. "Let's shake hands on that decision, shall we?"

So David shook hands gravely, thinking as he did so that here was a man he would do anything in the world to please. Next, Mr. Lincoln held out his hand to Nancy.

"You've a fine brother here, young lady," he said, as she laid her hand in his. "I think he'll make you very proud of him someday."

Nancy nodded. It was on the tip of her tongue to say that David had already made his family proud of him by his rescue of Jim. But before the words could leave her mouth, Abraham Lincoln patted her on the shoulder, swung around on his heel, and strode across the hall to join his friends, who were awaiting him impatiently.

Together, David and Nancy left the Wigwam and started home. They had walked a full block before either one of them spoke. Then Nancy sighed happily. "He's just as nice as I thought he was when he came into the shop that day," she murmured. "I wish Mother and Grandfather and the boys could have been with us."

"I wish Jim could have, too," David said. "Lots of times when we were helping build the Wigwam, we used to wonder if Mr. Lincoln would ever come to look at it."

Nancy glanced sideways at her brother. "Did you really mean that about going back to school?"

"Of course I did!" David exclaimed stoutly. "I reckon I won't like it any better than I used to, but I'm going back tomorrow morning, just the same. Don't you tell Grandpa and Ma about it, though, will you? I want to do that myself, as soon as we get home."

For one reason or another, it was evening and supper was almost ready before Nancy and David had a chance to tell the family about their meeting with Abraham Lincoln. Robbie and Peter listened to the story, wide-eyed, and asked all sorts of questions. Mother said she felt very proud that two of *her* children had talked to the man who was to be the next President of the United States. But Grandfather never spoke a word until David had told about the dictionary and announced that he was returning to the Dearborn School the very next day.

"Humph!" said Grandfather. "I always knew you'd come to your senses some day, lad, but I never dreamed it would take Abraham Lincoln to bring you around."

The old gentleman spoke rather gruffly, but his eyes twinkled. David could tell by the expression on his face that he was pleased. And Mother beamed at him happily as she called the family to the supper table.

"Now, if only Jim weren't going to be so far away, everything would be fine," David thought as he sat down and bowed his head, waiting for Grandfather to ask the blessing.

"Bless this food, dear Lord," Grandfather began in his deep voice. Then, disturbed by a noise close by, he opened his eyes. "Peter," he said sternly to the small boy who had slipped from his chair and was halfway across the kitchen, "come back to your place at once."

"But Grandpa," Peter protested. "I heard someone knock. I know I did." And before Grandfather could say anything more, he pulled open the door.

"Jim!" he cried in his shrill little voice. "It's Jim!"

And there in the doorway, cap in one hand and bag in the other, was Jim. David sprang up so suddenly that his chair fell over with a clatter.

"What's the matter?" he asked, hardly daring to believe his eyes. "Did Captain Clark throw you off the boat?"

Jim shook his head. "No," he said, coming into the room. "He didn't throw me off. I just got to thinkin' this afternoon, while I was peelin' potatoes in the galley. I was born here in this country, Dave, same as you were. It's my home, an' — well, I figure you and me, workin' together, can lick all the Snivelys an' —"

David drew a deep breath, and his eyes were shining. "You mean you aren't going to Canada?" he cried excitedly. "You mean you're not going?"

Jim nodded. "That's right," he said with a slow grin.

"Hurray!" yelled David, grabbing his friend by the arms. "Robbie! Nancy! Jim's staying! Move over. Move over, everybody. We've got to make a place for Jim."

"Yes," agreed Grandfather, smiling at the boys. "We must all move over and make a place for Jim."